"This Is *My* Baby, Cole,"

Regan said.

"*Mine*. I'd already planned on being a single mother, which is why I went to be inseminated. I have no intention of shuttling my child back and forth between me and the father. That's not what I want for my baby."

"*Our* baby," he corrected her. "And I agree completely."

"Does that mean you…that you will relinquish your rights and let me raise the baby?"

Her words hit him like blows. After all, it wasn't the first time he hadn't been found good enough, he reminded himself. In her eyes, for a child to have no father would be preferable than to have him as one. "Sorry to disappoint you, princess, but that's not what I had in mind. I think a child belongs with both parents."

"But that's not possible."

"Sure it is. All we have to do is get married."

Dear Reader,

Twenty years ago in May, the first Silhouette romance was published, and in 2000 we're celebrating our 20th anniversary all year long! Celebrate with us—and start with six powerful, passionate, provocative love stories from Silhouette Desire.

Elizabeth Bevarly offers a MAN OF THE MONTH so tempting that we decided to call it *Dr. Irresistible!* Enjoy this sexy tale about a single-mom nurse who enlists a handsome doctor to pose as her husband at her tenth high school reunion. The wonderful miniseries LONE STAR FAMILIES: THE LOGANS, by bestselling author Leanne Banks, continues with *Expecting His Child,* a sensual romance about a woman carrying the child of her family's nemesis after a stolen night of passion.

Ever-talented Cindy Gerard returns to Desire with *In His Loving Arms,* in which a pregnant widow is reunited with the man who's haunted her dreams for seven years. Sheikhs abound in Alexandra Sellers' *Sheikh's Honor,* a new addition to her dramatic miniseries SONS OF THE DESERT. The Desire theme promotion, THE BABY BANK, about women who find love unexpectedly when seeking sperm donors, continues with Metsy Hingle's *The Baby Bonus.* And new-comer Kathie DeNosky makes her Desire debut with *Did You Say Married?!,* in which the heroine wakes up in Vegas next to a sexy cowboy who turns out to be her newly wed husband.

What a lineup! So this May, for Mother's Day, why not treat your mom—and yourself—to all six of these highly sensual and emotional love stories from Silhouette Desire!

Enjoy!

Joan Marlow Golan

Joan Marlow Golan
Senior Editor, Silhouette Desire

Please address questions and book requests to:
Silhouette Reader Service
U.S.: 3010 Walden Ave., P.O. Box 1325, Buffalo, NY 14269
Canadian: P.O. Box 609, Fort Erie, Ont. L2A 5X3

The Baby Bonus
METSY HINGLE

Silhouette®

Desire

Published by Silhouette Books
America's Publisher of Contemporary Romance

For Jimmy and Julie Hingle,
my darling son and his lovely wife,
and their very special "Baby Bonus,"
Caroline Josephine Hingle

SILHOUETTE BOOKS

ISBN 0-373-76295-X

THE BABY BONUS

Visit Silhouette at www.eHarlequin.com

Printed in U.S.A.

Books by Metsy Hingle

Silhouette Desire

Seduced #900
Surrender #978
Backfire #1026
Lovechild #1055
The Kidnapped Bride #1103
Switched at the Altar #1133
The Bodyguard and the Bridesmaid #1146
Dad in Demand #1241
Secret Agent Dad #1250
†*The Baby Bonus* #1295

*Right Bride, Wrong Groom
†The Baby Bank

METSY HINGLE

celebrates her tenth book for Silhouette with the publication of *The Baby Bonus*. Metsy is an award-winning, best-selling author of romance who resides across the lake from her native New Orleans. Married for more than twenty years to her own hero, she is the busy mother of four children. She recently traded in her business suits and a fast-paced life in the hotel and public-relations arena to pursue writing full-time. Metsy has a strong belief in the power of love and romance. She also believes in happy endings, which she continues to demonstrate with each new story she writes. She loves hearing from readers. For a free doorknob hanger or bookmark, write to Metsy at P.O. Box 3224, Covington, LA 70433.

IT'S OUR 20th ANNIVERSARY!
We'll be celebrating all year,
Continuing with these fabulous titles,
On sale in May 2000.

Romance

#1444 Mercenary's Woman
Diana Palmer

#1445 Too Hard To Handle
Rita Rainville

#1446 A Royal Mission
Elizabeth August

#1447 Tall, Strong & Cool Under Fire
Marie Ferrarella

#1448 Hannah Gets a Husband
Julianna Morris

#1449 Her Sister's Child
Lilian Darcy

Desire

#1291 Dr. Irresistible
Elizabeth Bevarly

#1292 Expecting His Child
Leanne Banks

#1293 In His Loving Arms
Cindy Gerard

#1294 Sheikh's Honor
Alexandra Sellers

#1295 The Baby Bonus
Metsy Hingle

#1296 Did You Say Married?!
Kathie DeNosky

Intimate Moments

#1003 Rogue's Reform
Marilyn Pappano

#1004 The Cowboy's Hidden Agenda
Kathleen Creighton

#1005 In a Heartbeat
Carla Cassidy

#1006 Anything for Her Marriage
Karen Templeton

#1007 Every Little Thing
Linda Winstead Jones

#1008 Remember the Night
Linda Castillo

Special Edition

#1321 The Kincaid Bride
Jackie Merritt

#1322 The Millionaire She Married
Christine Rimmer

#1323 Warrior's Embrace
Peggy Webb

#1324 The Sheik's Arranged Marriage
Susan Mallery

#1325 Sullivan's Child
Gail Link

#1326 Wild Mustang
Jane Toombs

Prologue

"I'm pregnant?" Regan St. Claire repeated, her nails digging into the palms of her hands. She stared across the desk at her aunt, New Orleans' noted fertility specialist, Dr. Elizabeth St. Claire. "You're sure, Aunt Liz? I mean there's no mistake?"

The older woman shook her silvery-blond head and smiled. "I'm sure. Ran the tests myself—twice. You're definitely pregnant, dear. Based on the date I performed the insemination procedure, you're just shy of five weeks along."

Regan squealed with delight. Too excited to sit still, she shot to her feet and raced around the desk to hug her aunt. "I'm going to have a baby! A baby," she said again in awe, dancing them both around in a circle.

"Regan, child. Slow down," her aunt admonished, laughter in her voice.

"I can't. I'm too happy," she countered, tears of joy stinging her eyes. Even now she could hardly believe that a diagnosis of endometriosis and possible infertility had spurred her down this path that had resulted in a…a miracle. Because that's what this baby was. A miracle. "I've wanted a baby for so long. Ever since…" Ever since she had miscarried her first child—Cole's child—all those years ago.

As though reading her thoughts, her aunt offered her hand. Regan clasped it, drew strength from the woman who had filled the role of mother for nearly all of her twenty-nine years. "Honey, it's still early days," Aunt Liz cautioned. "That tiny life inside you has a long way to go before he or she makes a debut."

"I know," Regan replied, her smile slipping a notch as she recalled her last pregnancy. She'd been seventeen and madly in love with Cole Thornton. As if it were only yesterday instead of twelve years ago, images of Cole filled her mind's eye. Cole working in her family's garden, sweat glistening on his sun-darkened skin, muscles rippling across his bare shoulders as he sank a shovel into the soil. Cole lifting his head, swiping the midnight hair from his face and staring at her out of those silver eyes.

There had been something wild and dangerous in his eyes when he'd looked at her. He'd been so different from the boys she knew—so serious and driven, so much smoldering passion. She'd been drawn to him instantly. After getting to know him, she'd admired his strong sense of honor and determination to make something of himself. But it had been the yearning to belong that she sensed in Cole that had stolen her heart. Making love with him had been as elemental as breathing to her. When she'd become pregnant, he had insisted they marry—just as she'd known he would. Convincing him to elope had been the tricky part. Yet, even after all this time, she remembered those magical days as his wife— days when she'd been so sure their love was strong enough to survive anything.

Until her world came crashing down, and she'd lost both Cole and their baby.

"…and I just hope that…that I've done the right thing. You mean the world to me, Regan. All I want…all I've ever wanted is for you to be happy."

Something in her aunt's tone snagged Regan's attention, pulled her from thoughts about the past. "I *am* happy, Aunt Liz. You've given me the one thing in the world that I want most—a baby…or at least the chance to have a baby."

A worried frown chased across her aunt's brow. "As wonderful as a baby is, it only fills a part of your life. What about a husband? Someone to share your life with? Don't you want someone to be a father to this baby, to make more babies with you?"

Regan sighed at her aunt's simple assessment of all the things missing in her life. "You didn't need a man to make your life complete, Aunt Liz. Neither do I."

"We're not talking about me, dear. Besides, I did have someone once. Someone I was foolish enough to let go. I'm an old woman now, with most of my life behind me. But you…you have most of your life still ahead of you. Don't waste it. Don't settle for memories and regrets."

"I'm not wasting my life," Regan insisted.

"Are you sure? I can't help remembering the last time you were pregnant. How happy and in love you and Cole were, and when the two of you got married—"

"Our marriage was a mistake. We were too young to know what we were doing."

Her aunt's frown deepened. The brown eyes so like her father's pinned her. "You were old enough to know that you loved each other, to conceive a child together. I've often wondered if your father hadn't insisted on that annulment—"

"Daddy did what he thought was best," Regan countered, a lump forming in her throat. She turned away, stared out the window, hugging her arms about her as though it could somehow stop the ache that always came when she played the game of what-ifs. What if she had gone to Cole and told him about her father's threats to have him arrested because she'd been underage unless she annulled the marriage? What if she hadn't lied to Cole, hadn't said she didn't love him? What if…

"Honey, I know you loved your father. He was my brother, and I loved him too. But that doesn't mean I was blind to his faults. He wasn't perfect. Sometimes he made mistakes, judged people unfairly. He was wrong about Cole. And he was wrong to interfere in your marriage, to force you to make a choice."

"What's done is done, Aunt Liz. We can't go back." Determined to lock the painful door to the past, she turned around to face her aunt. "What matters is the future. This baby is my future."

"You're right," her aunt said, sliding a worried glance to Regan's stomach. "I just hope that whatever happens…"

Suddenly alarmed, Regan placed her hand protectively on her belly. Fear curled like a fist around her heart. "Aunt Liz, is there something you haven't told me? Is there…is there something wrong with my baby?"

"No. Oh no, child. Nothing's wrong with the baby."

"Then what is it? Why the long face?"

She shook her head, gave her a tight smile. "I guess I'm just worrying that maybe I'm as bad as your father because I'm the one interfering in your life now."

Relief washed through Regan. "You haven't. You've given me a priceless gift."

"But what if—"

"No what-ifs," Regan insisted. "Everything's going to be fine. Just wait and see. This time absolutely nothing's going to go wrong."

One

Absolutely everything seemed to be going wrong, Regan admitted as she retraced her path from the ladies' room to her office at the rear of the jewelry salon. Pressing a hand to her still-queasy stomach, she eased behind the worktable where her jeweler's tools, an assortment of gems and several pieces awaited her attention.

"Come on, Slugger," Regan pleaded, smoothing her palm over her still-flat belly. "How about giving Mommy a break here? Morning sickness is called that for a reason. These tummy hijinks are not supposed to happen in the afternoon, too." She certainly hadn't expected the morning sickness to plague her long and late into every day, as had been the case during the two weeks since she'd confirmed her pregnancy. Nor had she expected her energy level to dip so drastically that it rivaled New Orleans' below-sea-level position along the Mississippi River. Sighing, Regan shook her head. This pregnancy was so different from the last one, she thought, and immediately regretted the comparison as memories of the miscarriage came flooding back.

Squeezing her eyes shut a moment, Regan pressed a fist against the ache in her heart—an ache that time had dulled but never quite healed. She sucked in a breath and tried to banish the pain that always accompanied thoughts of that sad time in her life. Things were different now, she reminded herself. *She* was different. She wasn't a starry-eyed girl unexpectedly pregnant with her lover's child this time. She was a woman, without any foolish illusions about love. This pregnancy was the result of planning, not passion. And in just over seven months when she held her baby in her arms, she would have everything she wanted, everything she needed.

What about a husband? Someone to share your life with? Someone to be a father to this baby?

Her aunt's words replayed in Regan's head, taunting her. Ruthlessly, she shut them off. Aunt Liz was wrong, she assured herself. She didn't need or want a husband. All she needed was her baby, a child of her own to hold in her arms, to give all the love she had stored in her heart. Patting her tummy, she whispered, "Don't worry, sweetie. We'll be just fine. You'll see. You won't even miss not having a daddy because I'm going to be the best mommy possible. I promise."

The wink of diamonds caught her eye, and Regan glanced at the jewelry spread out before her in various stages of completion. Becoming mommy of the year would have to wait a bit longer, she decided. Right now, she had work to do—work that the store desperately needed if she hoped to make the mortgage payment on time this month. Thoughts of the hefty mortgage made her frown, and, not for the first time, Regan wished she had taken a few business courses along with her classes on gem-cutting and grading. Heaven knows she certainly could have used even just a little of what she had once considered the dull business know-how during this past year. But then, she'd had no idea she would ever need to worry about things like fiscal management and market share and interest rates. She certainly had never dreamed that she would find herself in a financial mess and in danger of losing the store that had been in her family for five generations. And while she'd managed to hang on so far, she wasn't out of the woods by any means. Flicking on the work light, she repositioned the sketch she'd made of a ring, but her thoughts drifted once more to her finances.

You should have told me we were in trouble, Daddy. Why didn't you at least let me try to help?

But she knew why her father hadn't told her, Regan admitted. He had been protecting her—as he always did. Anger sparked anew as she recalled the dual shocks of her father's sudden death and the discovery that Exclusives was on the verge of bankruptcy. But on the heels of her resentment came guilt. She had no right to be angry with her father— not when he'd given her so much. After all, it had been her father who had introduced her to the magical world of gems and nurtured her dreams of designing. Maybe he had been overprotective at times, but only because he had loved her. And he had been there when she needed him, had helped her pick up the pieces of her life when she'd lost both her baby and Cole. She owed it to her father to make the store solvent again, to pass on the legacy to her own child some-day. And she would, Regan vowed. "I won't let you down, Daddy," she promised.

Swiping at the tears that seemed to surface so easily these days, Regan picked up the ring she'd been working on before her dash to the bathroom. "What do you say, Slugger? No more shenanigans until I finish this piece. All right?"

When her stomach had remained calm for a full five minutes, Regan grinned. Evidently, she and Slugger had worked out a deal. She glanced at the sketch and then at the ring and frowned. Running a fingertip along the gold band, an anniversary gift for one of the store's best clients, she studied the piece with a critical eye. The four-carat Burmese ruby at the center of the ring was exquisite, she conceded, admiring the brilliant luster of the stone, the way it caught and reflected the light. Despite its size and origin, the silk effect, or straw inclusions, so common in rubies were so faint they were invisible to the naked eye. The diamond baguettes flanking either side of the blood-red gem set off the ruby perfectly. The ring was beautiful, and the customer would be very happy with it. Yet, Regan itched to replace the ruby with the fiery green emerald locked in the safe.

"Your mommy's crazy, Slugger," she muttered. Selling the ruby would be the smart thing to do, not to mention far more lucrative since it was a more expensive stone. But the part of her that had always been drawn to the magic of the stones rather than to their monetary value kept seeing the emerald nestled between the diamonds. The fact that the heart stone, as the emerald was known, would be all the more fitting for the occasion only compounded her desire to use it. Regan sighed again. Not only was she crazy, she decided, pushing back from her worktable, but she was a lousy businesswoman to boot. Walking across the room, she unlocked the vault and retrieved a black velvet tray of gems. She'd just placed the tray on her worktable when the intercom on the desk behind her buzzed.

"Ms. St. Claire?"

Turning, Regan hit the speaker button on the phone. "Yes, Amy," she replied, wishing the new receptionist would call her Regan as she had asked her to do.

"There's a Mr. Cole Thornton here to see you."

Regan froze. Suddenly the air backed up in her lungs. Her stomach did a nosedive, and the room began to spin. Her knees wobbly, she sank down onto the chair beside the desk and tried to suck in a breath.

Cole Thornton. Here in New Orleans. To see her? After all this time?

Twelve years had passed since that horrible day when

he'd looked at her with ice in his gray eyes as he'd lashed out at her before leaving town. He'd never spoken to her again. Not once. But she had never forgotten him. How could she when the city that had once shunned the dirt-poor young Cole was so eager to claim the successful real-estate mogul as one of its native sons? She'd lost count of the photos she'd seen of him at various business and charity functions over the years—the snippets of gossip about his latest acquisitions, the lavish parties he attended, the glamorous women he dated. As far as she knew, until now, he'd only returned to New Orleans once. Recalling her brief encounter with him on that one occasion still stung. Just remembering his cool indifference, the way he'd looked right through her sent a stab of pain through her. No way did she intend to put herself through that kind of anguish again. Especially not now.

"Ms. St. Claire? Should I send Mr. Thornton in?"

"No," Regan shot back. Swallowing past the tightness in her throat, she assured herself that this rush of emotion she was experiencing was due to her pregnancy and had nothing to do with any lingering feelings she had for Cole. "Please give Mr. Thornton my apologies, Amy, and tell him I'm unavailable. Oh and, Amy, I'd appreciate it if you'd hold my calls," she said before severing the connection.

Feeling a bit unsteady, Regan returned to her worktable and sank down to her stool. Think of work, she commanded herself. Work had been her refuge twelve years ago. It would be her refuge now. Besides, she reminded herself, she had a baby on the way and a staff who needed her to make sure Exclusives stayed afloat. Intent on removing the ruby from its setting, Regan didn't even bother looking up when she heard the door open a few minutes later. "Whatever it is, Amy, I'll deal with it later. I don't have time right now."

"Then I suggest you make time."

The tool fell from Regan's fingers and clattered noisily

on the marble tabletop, at the sound of the voice that had once sent shivers of longing up her spine.

"Ms. St. Claire, I'm sorry," a nervous Amy said as she rushed in behind Cole. Her eyes shifted anxiously from Regan to Cole and back again. "I tried to explain to Mr. Thornton that you couldn't see him—"

"And I assured Amy that you *would* see me," Cole replied.

"It's all right, Amy," Regan told the young woman in a voice that belied the fact that her heart was slamming against her ribs. "I'll handle it."

Amy didn't need to be told twice. She scurried out of the room, pulling the door closed behind her. And as she watched the other woman escape, Regan fervently wished she could do the same. Bracing herself, she met Cole's gaze.

"And just how do you plan to handle me, princess?"

Regan gritted her teeth at his use of the pet name he'd saddled her with years ago. Trying to instill ice in her voice she asked, "What do you want, Cole?"

His eyes darkened, gleamed a liquid silver, sparking memories of the nights she'd lain naked in his arms. He arched a brow. "Should I consider that an invitation?"

Color flashed up Regan's cheeks, and she cursed her fair skin when she saw his lips twist into a smile. "Hardly," she replied. Oh God, it simply wasn't fair. At thirty-three, Cole was even more handsome now than he'd been at twenty-one. His hair was shorter, but just as thick and still as dark as midnight. There were faint lines etched at the corners of his eyes that hadn't been there twelve years ago, lines that made him look harder, colder, she thought. But his eyes were still that same incredible shade of gray capable of going from frost to molten silver in an instant. His long lean body didn't sport any extra pounds that she could detect, and she'd lay odds that the muscles beneath his designer shirt and suit were still as hard as steel. Unable to stop herself, she stared at his mouth—the mouth that had kissed her with such hunger, had tasted every inch of her body, had whispered promises of love.

"You still blush like a schoolgirl, princess," he told her. "How is that possible?"

Flustered, Regan stood. "I don't have time for games, Cole. I have a business to run. So why don't you tell me why you're here?"

His mouth hardened a moment, but instead of answering, he perched himself on the edge of her table and picked up the ring she'd been working on. "Far be it from me to waste your valuable time. After all," he said, looking from the ring to her, "I know firsthand what a high priority you place on business. That's why I'm here. To discuss business."

The word *business* hit Regan like a slap. Immediately she recalled the gorgeous redhead who had accompanied him to the fundraiser at the city's aquarium last year. Regan's business, her primary business, was designing one-of-a-kind rings for Exclusives. Her throat grew tight. He couldn't possibly expect her to design a ring for his lover, she told herself. Not even Cole would be that cruel.

Unless he felt he had a reason to be cruel. And, in Cole's eyes, he believed he had a reason. He thought she had betrayed him. It didn't matter that she hadn't. He'd never believed her when she'd come to him later and tried to explain the reasons she'd had their marriage annulled, that she'd done it to save him. The result had been the same. She'd hurt him, had ripped his pride to shreds at a time when pride was all he'd had. What better payback than to commission her to design his future wife's wedding ring? Regan stared at the ring in Cole's hand and recalled the day he'd placed a thin gold band on her finger and promised to love her always. *Always* had only lasted ten days. Pain sliced through Regan, razor-sharp, at the memory. Deserving or not and no matter how badly she could use the sale and publicity, she refused to subject herself to that kind of misery. "As I said, I'm very busy. I'll get my assistant to help you."

"Like hell you will!" Quick as a snap he was off the table and in her face. "I'm not dealing with any assistant on something this important. I'm dealing with *you*, princess. And only you."

Staggered by his sudden shift from cool control to white-hot fury, Regan took a step back. Emotions tumbled through her at breakneck speed, and she recalled the other two times she'd seen Cole in the grips of a temper like this—the day she'd told him she wanted an annulment and the day she'd told him she'd lost their baby. She drew in a calming breath. "I'd like you to leave."

A muscle twitched in his jaw. "What's the matter, princess? Changed your mind again? It's a little late for that now, don't you think?"

Regan frowned, confused as much by Cole's remarks as by his hostility. "I don't know what you're talking about, and, to tell you the truth, I don't really care. I just want you to go."

"Not a chance."

Regan's pulse danced uneasily at the steely determination in his voice. "Then you leave me no choice but to call the police and have you removed," she said with more conviction than she felt. She started toward the phone, when suddenly Slugger decided he hadn't finished playing games for the day. Her stomach dipped. A wave of nausea rolled through her. "Excuse me," she mumbled, and tried to move past Cole before she lost what was left of her lunch in front of him.

Cole blocked her path. "I don't think so. Not until we talk."

"Get out of my way," she commanded, fighting back the nausea climbing up her throat. "I mean it, Cole. Get out of my way, or you're going to be sorry."

"Sorrier than you were twelve years ago when you real-ized what a mistake you made by marrying a poor bastard?

Oh, I forgot, my being a bastard isn't quite so bad now that I have money, is it?''

For a moment the dots in front of her eyes cleared, as the full measure of his bitterness hit her. Regan blinked back the tears of anger and hurt stinging her eyes. ''Go to hell.''

''No thanks, sweetheart, I've already been there once because of you. And I have no intention of going back. In fact, now that you're pregnant, I—''

The shock of his words hit Regan like a punch, and on its heels came another wave of nausea. She clamped one hand over her mouth and used the other to shove past him. Cole caught her shoulder, pulled her around to face him. Then it was too late. She upchucked all over his expensive black shoes.

Stunned, Cole stood frozen for several seconds. As he battled through the anger that had gripped him at Regan's dismissal, he registered her paper-white pallor, the beads of sweat dotting her brow.

''I'm sorry,'' she muttered, a horrified expression on her face, before she broke free and fled.

''Regan, wait,'' Cole shouted, charging after her. He skidded to a halt when the bathroom door swung shut, barely missing his nose. He pounded on the door with his fist. ''Regan!''

''Go away!''

Concerned, he twisted the doorknob, found the thing locked. ''Open the door, Regan.''

''Go away!''

Not a chance. Liz hadn't told him that she was sick. Regan never got sick—at least not that he could remember. Even during her short pregnancy years ago, she hadn't suffered so much as an hour of morning sickness. She hadn't been sick a single day—until the miscarriage.

Suddenly the idea that Regan and his baby could be in any danger had the blood chilling in his veins. Damn! He should never have baited her the way he had, recalling the way the color had drained from her cheeks when he'd lashed out at her. He washed a hand down his face, shamed by his actions. Worse, he was scared. If something happened to her or the baby, it would be *his* fault. His insides suddenly churning, Cole raised his fist but forced himself to tap on the door, gently this time. "Princess? Are you all right?"

When she didn't answer, Cole knocked again. Guilt and worry played havoc in his mind as he envisioned Regan lying on the bathroom floor helpless, maybe in pain. "Princess, can you hear me?" he asked, growing more anxious by the second. "Unlock the door. Let me in so I can help you."

When she still failed to respond, the knot of fear in his stomach balled into a fist. Cole tried the doorknob again, gave it a menacing twist. Then he heard it—that terrible wretching sound of someone being sick. On the heels of that came a soft moan and then the sound of running water. He shoved at the door, contemplated kicking the thing in. "Are you all right?" he demanded, nerves making his voice sharp, his temper short. "Dammit, Regan, answer me."

"I'm all right."

But she didn't sound all right. She sounded as weak as a newborn kitten. Sucking in a calming breath, Cole attempted to rein in the jumble of emotions racing through him. "Open the door, princess," he coaxed, deliberately gentling his voice even though inside he felt raw, violent. "I know you're sick. Please…open the door. Let me help you."

"I don't want your help," she tossed back with more spirit than he'd expected. "I just want you to leave."

Too bad, Cole thought, gritting his teeth. No way did he plan to leave—not until he was sure that she was okay. And the baby, he amended. After all, the baby was the reason he was here in the first place. Raking a hand through his hair, Cole sighed. According to *Money* magazine he was a smart man, a virtual business genius. So how the devil had he gotten himself into this mess? How the devil had he let himself get tangled up with Regan St. Claire again?

The answer was simple—Liz, his oldest and dearest friend, the woman who had taken a street-smart, angry punk under her wing and given him a chance to be something more. He owed her more than he could ever repay in one lifetime. But hell, this time Regan's aunt Liz had gone too far.

And whose fault is that?

His, Cole admitted. Because he had only himself to blame for getting into this fix in the first place. After all, he knew how clever Liz was, and he also knew how much the woman loved her niece. Liz had known exactly which buttons to push to convince him to be Regan's sperm donor. And idiot that he was, he'd fallen right into the trap....

"Forget it, Liz. If Regan needs a sperm donor, you'll have to find someone else. Maybe one of those uptowners with the mile-long pedigrees."

"Fine," Liz agreed easily.

Too easily, he thought. The woman was as sharp as a tack and never gave up that easily. Narrowing his gaze, he looked at her, knowing instinctively she was up to something. *"I mean it, Liz."*

"I said okay, didn't I?"

"But?"

"But what?" she asked innocently.

Cole sighed. *"Whatever it is you've got up your sleeve isn't going to work."*

"You make me sound like a scheming manipulative woman."

"That's because sometimes you are, but I love you anyway."

She sniffed, tipped up her nose.

"Why don't you just spit out whatever it is you're up to?"

"I'm disappointed in you, Cole Thornton. I never thought

you'd let pigheaded pride stand in the way and stop you from having the one thing you've always wanted.''

Cole laughed. *''If you think I'm still pining after Regan, you've been standing too close to the ether, doc. Getting tangled up with your niece once was enough for me. Believe me, I have no desire to repeat that mistake.''* Certainly not when he still bore the scars from their short-lived union.

Her brown eyes twinkled in a way that said *''gotcha.'' ''Isn't it interesting that you thought I was referring to Regan?''*

Cole scowled, annoyed as much with himself as with Liz.

''I was referring to a baby. More specifically, your baby.'' Her expression sobered. *''I remember how devastated you were when…when Regan miscarried. I know how much you wanted that baby, how much you were looking forward to becoming a father.''*

Pain ripped through Cole at the reminder of that dreadful day when Regan had told him she'd lost their baby. Even after all this time, it hurt to think of his child, his little girl, that had never had a chance to live, that he had never had a chance to hold. *''Leave it alone, Liz.''*

She reached out, touched his hand. *''For whatever reason, fate stole your and Regan's daughter, Cole. Nothing can ever change that. But don't you see? If you helped Regan now, it could be a second chance for both of you.''*

Memories crowding him, Cole pulled away. *''There are no second chances, Liz.''*

She frowned. *''Careful, Cole. You're beginning to sound a lot like my brother. I'd hate to see you end up like Philip. Despite all his blessings, he was an unhappy and lonely man until the day he died.''*

''I'm nothing like him,'' Cole snapped, insulted to be compared to the man he'd once admired and whose approval he'd struggled so hard to win; the man who had been his employer and, briefly, his father-in-law. The man he'd grown to hate so fiercely that he'd spent the past dozen years

of his life working like a madman just to prove how wrong Philip St. Claire had been about him.

"Are you sure? You're rich and successful just as you swore you'd be, but I don't see that it's made you happy."

"I'm happy."

"Then why are you still alone? And why in all the news clippings I see of you with one beautiful woman after another on your arm, why doesn't the smile on your lips reach your eyes? For all my brother's sins, he at least had Regan. She was the best part of him, and worth a hundred times more than all of his priceless jewels. She brought love and laughter into Philip's life, and now that he's gone, she's carrying on his legacy. What about you, Cole? You have the power and fortune you always wanted, but what else do you have? Who do you have to bring love and laughter into your life? Who do you have to carry on your legacy when you're gone?"

The reminder of how empty his life was staggered Cole, yet he refused to admit that fact to Liz. Instead, he hardened his jaw and met her eyes. "I don't need love in my life. I stopped believing in it a long time ago. As for the rest, if and when I decide I want someone, I'll buy them."

Liz shook her head, her expression sad. "And you say you're not like Philip?"

Suddenly the image of Philip St. Claire trying to buy him out of Regan's life came rushing back. Angry, Cole snapped, "I'm not like him. I don't judge people by their pedigrees and bank accounts. I may have made mistakes, but I own up to them and I learn from them. Marrying Regan was the biggest mistake I ever made, and I have enough sense not to repeat it."

Liz arched her brow. "Funny. I don't recall mentioning the word marriage. All I was suggesting was that you be Regan's sperm donor. Obviously, I was wrong in thinking that the idea of becoming a father would appeal to you. So, *please, don't give it another thought. I'll just find someone else.''*

Only she hadn't had to find someone else. Because *he* had taken the bait—fallen into the trap. The momentary madness that saw him agree to Liz's outrageous plan had lasted a full month. But by the time the folly of his actions had set in, he'd been in Europe and knee-deep in sensitive negotiations. He'd put off making the call to Liz, reasoning that he'd have time to take care of everything and tell Liz he had changed his mind when he got back. After all, he'd read all the data. He knew that the chance of the insemination procedure working on the first try was at best thirty percent. He'd thought he had time, and he'd put off making that call to Liz.

Big mistake, Thornton. You should have followed through, called Liz the minute you'd changed your mind and had her destroy the sperm sample.

But he hadn't followed through—a mistake he seldom made in business. Not for the first time, Cole cursed his own carelessness. He had no one to blame for this mess but himself. He'd known Liz had an agenda. He just hadn't anticipated how quickly she would set it into motion or that she would be successful on the first try. Nor had he anticipated, returning after a grueling trip, the news that Regan was already pregnant—with *his* child.

''What a mess,'' Cole muttered. Still suffering from jet lag, he rolled his shoulders, tried to work out some of the kinks. After getting Liz's message earlier, he hadn't even bothered unpacking. He'd simply boarded a plane for New Orleans, determined to talk with Regan and figure out a way to straighten out the mess they'd gotten themselves into.

Only his partner in this particular mess was now locked in the bathroom puking her guts out. Cole listened at the door and was relieved not to hear any more wretching or moaning, just the sound of Regan moving about the room. Satisfied she was in no danger, he looked down at his soiled shoes and winced, then retreated to the kitchen to see what could be done to salvage them.

After cleaning off his shoes as best he could, Cole tackled the spot where Regan had missed him and caught the carpet instead. The entire job took no more than a few minutes. Since she still hadn't emerged from the bathroom, he headed back to her office area to wait.

He didn't have to wait long. Ten minutes later Regan left the bathroom. She did a quick scan of the spacious area that made up the offices and design quarters of Exclusives. Apparently satisfied, she headed for the kitchen at the rear of the big room. She hadn't seen him, Cole realized, as he straightened from beside the worktable where he'd stooped down to retrieve an emerald that must have fallen on the floor when she'd rushed past him. Closing his fingers around the glittering green stone, he watched Regan put the kettle on top of the stove and begin to prepare herself a cup of tea. He should announce his presence, Cole told himself, feeling like a voyeur. Yet, he remained silent.

In the dozen years since she had ripped out his heart and made a fool of him, he'd been with other women. Women far more beautiful than Regan St. Claire, women with blood-lines and fortunes far more impressive than hers. Yet, not one of those women had ever been able to make his blood heat or his body grow hard the way Regan did now—just as she had the very first time he'd seen her. She'd been seated on the veranda of her family home watching him plant azaleas. And then she'd smiled at him. The impact of that shy smile had hit him like a sucker punch, stealing his breath, making him ache, making him want. Even after all this time and all that she'd done, that one thing hadn't changed. All he had to do was look at Regan to want her. He'd wanted her a year ago when he'd seen her at some charity gala he'd been roped into attending in the city. Only sheer force of will had enabled him to walk away and ignore her.

He didn't ignore her now. Instead he feasted on her with his eyes. Unguarded, without the polite mask she so often wore, Regan didn't look much different now than she had at seventeen. Oh, her figure was slightly fuller, more curvy than it had been, but not by much. Just enough to make her more tempting. From what he could determine, her taste in clothing hadn't changed. She still preferred silky, feminine things if that floral slip-like dress she had on was any indication. The way she carried herself hadn't changed either—like a princess—spine straight, shoulders back, head tilted at a proud angle. Staring at her face, he noted her skin was still porcelain-smooth, nearly translucent. Desire coiled inside him as he recalled the feel of that skin—whisper soft and sunshine warm.

Biting back a groan, Cole continued his appraisal, taking in her elegantly carved features—the high cheekbones, the patrician nose, the stubborn chin. Her wide-set eyes were the same fiery green he remembered—but there was a lingering sadness in those eyes now, shadows that dimmed the glow of her pregnancy. And he suspected those shadows didn't have a thing to do with her being sick.

Why so sad, Regan?

The answer came quickly—her father's death. It had been eight months since Philip St. Claire had died of a heart attack. And despite the fact that the man had been a ruthless SOB, Regan had idolized him. So much so that when forced to choose between them, she had chosen her father instead of him. Oh, he had told himself at the time that the money had been the deciding factor. He'd had none, and her father had had plenty. But deep down inside, Cole had known the truth. The novelty of tangling in the sheets with a bastard from the wrong side of the tracks had simply worn off, and Regan had realized she didn't love him after all.

Swallowing past the bitter memory, Cole stared at the woman who had been his wife, the woman who once again was pregnant with his child.

His child.

The impact of those words sent a surge of protectiveness through him. Suddenly the logical plan he'd hammered out on the flight from the west coast—the plan for sharing custody, for visitation schedules and arranging financial support—no longer seemed viable. He couldn't let this child be born illegitimate. How had he even thought for one moment that he could? Honor demanded that he do the responsible thing and marry Regan—if only temporarily. Liz had been right. He did want this child.

And the child's mother?

Cole skimmed his gaze over Regan again, noting how her thick blond braid fell over one shoulder to graze the curve of her breast. Heat stirred inside him again as he noted how her dress caressed the lines of her body, swirled around her calves. Dragging his attention back to her face, he stared at that sulky pink mouth. Unbidden, memories ambushed him—memories of those soft lips moving over his body, hot and eager. Desire already simmering, flared hot, curled tight and low in his groin, and he squeezed his eyes shut.

At the squeal of the kettle, Cole snapped his eyes open and cursed his own weakness. Despite Regan's betrayal, despite everything she had done, he still wanted her every bit as much now as he had twelve years ago. Maybe more. The admission angered him, frustrated him—especially since he realized now he'd only been kidding himself. He had *allowed* himself to fall into Liz's trap, for the simple reason that he'd never stopped wanting Regan.

And he would have her—her *and* their baby, he vowed silently. But first…first he had to convince Regan that marriage was their only option. With that thought in mind, Cole strode across the room to where she stood at the kitchen counter, stirring her tea. "Feeling better?"

Regan shrieked. The spoon flew from her fingers, clattered noisily as it hit the china. She spun around. "Cole," she gasped.

"Sorry. I didn't mean to frighten you."

"I—I thought you'd left."

"We need to talk."

"There isn't anything for us to talk about," she informed him and resumed preparation of her tea.

"What about the baby you're expecting?"

She hesitated a moment. "I assume Aunt Liz told you?"

"Of course, she told me. Did you think she wouldn't?"

"Well, she shouldn't have. After all, it certainly doesn't concern you."

"Is that so?" he asked, his voice deadly soft. Did she think he would walk away from his child? From his responsibilities?

Regan gave him a puzzled look. "Yes, that's so. Besides, why should you care if I'm pregnant? This time you had nothing to do with it."

The sneaking suspicion that had been prickling at the base of Cole's spine since Regan had refused to see him, suddenly curled around his throat like a hangman's noose. He scrubbed a hand down his face, feeling like a fool as the door to the trap Liz had set slammed firmly shut on them both. "I'm afraid that's where you're wrong, princess."

"W-what do you mean?" she asked, her eyes as wary as her voice.

"I mean that I had quite a lot to do with your being pregnant this time, too, because *I'm* the baby's father."

Two

"**N**o! I don't believe you. Aunt Liz would never do that to me," Regan insisted. Frantic, she prayed that was the truth…that her aunt had not put her…put either one of them in such an impossible position.

"Liz *did* do it to you. She did it to us *both*."

Regan shook her head. "No! She would have told me. I know she would."

Cole swore, jammed his hands through his hair. "I thought she *had* told you. But whether you like it or not, I *am* the father of the baby you're carrying."

It wasn't true. It couldn't be true. Panic racing through her, she blurted out, "You're lying. You have to be."

"Why the devil would I lie? What could I possibly hope to gain?"

"Vengeance," she replied without hesitation. "You hate me. You told me so the day I ended our marriage." As long as she lived, she would never forget the bitterness in Cole's voice when he'd thrown those words at her. Or the way she'd felt—as though he'd run a knife through her heart.

"I was angry at the time."

"You meant it." And he had. She had seen it in the way he'd looked at her with such utter contempt. Even now just the memory made her shudder.

"Can you blame me?" he snapped. "Can you? You were pregnant with my child. You had married me, sworn that you loved me, would always love me. But the minute your father showed up and threatened to cut your purse strings, all those pretty vows you took weren't worth spit. You high-tailed it home with daddy and left me."

"I told you later why I did it. I tried to explain—"

"You made excuses, princess. That's all they were. Excuses. The truth is that you liked the sex between us and needed to dress it up as love to justify what we did. But you didn't love me, and you didn't trust me to take care of you and our baby."

"Believe what you want." Defending herself against his accusations would be pointless. If he hadn't believed her twelve years ago, he certainly wouldn't believe her now. Besides, even if she did manage to convince him that he'd been wrong, what good would it do now? They couldn't go back and undo the past. Whatever love he'd felt for her—if it had indeed been love and not simply a mixture of lust and guilt over taking her innocence—those feelings had died the moment she'd told him she'd lost their baby. Even now, a chill went through her as she recalled Cole asking her if she'd lost his child or gotten rid of it. Shoving the crippling memory from her thoughts, Regan met his wintry gaze.

"I believe what your actions told me. The fact that you chose daddy and his money over me said plenty."

Not up to arguing with him, Regan shrugged. Feigning a calm she was far from feeling, she shifted her gaze away from those laser-sharp eyes and reached for her now-tepid cup of tea. She took a sip. The brew could have been dishwater for all she knew because her mouth tasted like ashes. "Which brings us back to my point. I bruised that monster-sized pride of yours, and you've never forgiven me for it. You swore someday I'd regret making a fool of you. Aunt Liz telling you about the baby and how I got pregnant would make it easy for you to pretend you're the father and certainly give you an opportunity to settle the score."

"Is that what you believe? That I'm settling a score?"

"Why should I believe otherwise? Even if Aunt Liz had asked you to be my sperm donor, we both know you would never have agreed. You hate me too much."

"Evidently not nearly as much as you seem to think," he said, his voice as tight as his expression. "Because you *are* pregnant, and it's *my* baby you're carrying."

Another flutter of panic twisted through her. Regan tightened her fingers around the cup she held. She didn't want to believe him, didn't dare believe him. "You're lying—"

"I'm telling you the truth," Cole countered, cutting off her denial. His expression thunderous, he moved closer, crowding her until her back nudged the kitchen counter.

She started to move away, but Cole's arm shot out, blocking her escape. Regan slapped her gaze up to his. And she went still at the cold determination in his eyes.

After a long moment, he said, "Liz told me about your problem a few months ago, and she did ask me to be a sperm donor. Foolishly, I agreed and until a few minutes ago I thought you had, too. But then, I guess I should have known better. Because you would never have wanted a man like me to father your baby, would you, princess?"

She didn't even bother dignifying his taunt with an answer.

"But the fact is it was *my* sperm Liz used. *Mine*. Unfortunately, you're just going to have to accept the fact that the baby you're carrying is mine."

He was telling her the truth. Even if the conviction in his

voice hadn't told her, she could read the truth in his cold, hard eyes.

She was carrying Cole's baby. Just like the last time. No, not like the last time. This time there was no love, no tenderness.

As the full measure of her predicament hit her, Regan's hands started to tremble. So did her legs. Suddenly the cheery lemon-and-white kitchen began to spin, and her body began to slide to the floor.

Cole swore. "Regan!"

On some level, Regan was aware of Cole snatching the wobbling cup from her fingers, of his strong arms wrapping around her, of him muttering something about crazy women. The colors in the room collided, turning into a sickly shade of gray. Then, as though in a dream, she felt herself being lifted, her head falling against his sturdy chest where a heart beat strong and fast beneath her fingertips.

And as she sank into the sea of gray that rushed up to swallow her, the last thing Regan remembered was the sound of Cole's voice whispering, "Come on. Open your eyes for me, princess."

At the sound of Cole's voice calling her princess, Regan fought her way back through the gray fog that had engulfed her.

"Come on. That's a girl. Open your eyes for me."

Slowly she lifted her heavy eyelids, her lashes fluttered once, twice, and finally Cole's face came into focus. His expression was grim, Regan noted and she caught a glimmer of alarm in his eyes. When the grip on her fingers tightened painfully, she realized that he was holding her hand.

"That's it," Cole murmured. He brushed a strand of hair away from her face, and he placed a cool, damp cloth on her forehead. "That's it. That's a good girl. Come on back now," he coaxed.

"W-what happened?"

"You fainted," he told her, his voice taut, his skin the color of paste.

"Sorry."

"Dammit, Regan, I don't want an apology. I..." He whooshed out a breath. "Are you all right?"

Regan blinked, taken aback by the concern in Cole's tone. Lord, if she didn't know better, she would actually think Cole cared about her. Just as quick as the thought came, she nipped it. That was one bridge she had no intention of buying. "I'm okay. I just got a little dizzy for a minute." She started to sit up.

"Stay put," he ordered, pressing a restraining hand against her shoulders. "There's an ambulance on the way and Liz is going to meet us at the hospital."

"What?" Regan slapped his hand away and sat up. Still slightly woozy, it took a moment before she realized that she was on the couch in her office. "You can just cancel that ambulance and tell my aunt not to bother going anywhere. Because I'm not going to the hospital."

"You're going."

"Think again, Thornton. No one tells me what to do— least of all you." She scooched herself up into a semi-sitting position and dragged in a calming breath. "Listen, I appreciate your concern. But there's nothing wrong with me. I'm fine."

"The hell you are!" Hands bunched into fists at his sides, Cole glared down at her. "You call tossing up your cookies and fainting fine?"

"No. I call it being pregnant," she informed him.

He eyed her warily as though she were some alien creature that he wasn't quite sure how to handle. Lord, but the man was a mess, Regan realized. He fit every cliché about expectant fathers that she'd ever heard of, from the off-color skin tone and panic-stricken eyes right down to the dark hair that looked as though he'd combed it with a rake. The last time she'd been pregnant, she couldn't remember him being so shaken. Not that she would have noticed. She'd been far too busy—first trying to convince Cole they should elope and then later trying to placate her father. But the poor guy was definitely shook up now, she thought, an amused smile curving her lips.

"I'm glad you think this is funny," the object of her musings snapped and rammed a fist through his already mussed hair. "You scared the hell out of me!"

"Sorry," she murmured, but she couldn't quite make herself feel remorse—not when her heart was still doing extra blips over the fact that Cole was actually worried about her. "I mean it. I really am sorry if I scared you. But please, no ambulance. Honestly, I feel fine now."

Cole shoved his hands into his pockets and huffed out a deep breath. "For Pete's sake. You're pregnant, princess. What if something…is wrong?"

"There's nothing wrong with me," she assured him.

"What about the baby?"

The momentary pleasure induced by his concern for her died swiftly. Of course, it wasn't *her* Cole was worried about. It was the baby. "There's nothing wrong with the baby. I'm pregnant, Cole. Sometimes pregnant women get nauseous and have dizzy spells."

"You don't. The last time…"

He didn't finish. He didn't need to. Because they both remembered that the last time she'd been pregnant she hadn't been sick at all. It wasn't until she'd missed her period for the third time that she'd even bought a test kit and confirmed her suspicions. To his credit, Cole hadn't hesitated to take responsibility. He'd insisted they get married right away. Oh, he had said all the right things that a seventeen-year-old girl needed to hear—that he loved her, that he would have asked her to marry him in a few years anyway, that they were just moving up the timetable a bit. Of course, she hadn't realized at the time how important it was to Cole that his child be born legitimate or that his insistence that they marry might have been due to her being pregnant and not because he loved her. She'd had plenty of time to figure that out later—after she'd lost the baby, after Cole had refused to listen to her pleas for a second chance, after he had left town and her for good.

"I still don't think you should take any chances."

"I don't intend to," she told him, pulling her thoughts back from the past. She stood and made her way over to the phone and buzzed her assistant. "Amy, please cancel the ambulance Mr. Thornton ordered and then notify my aunt that I'm all right and there's no need for her to go to the hospital." After assuring the other woman she was indeed fine, she hung up the phone and turned to face Cole.

"I want you to see a doctor," he informed her, a forbidding scowl on his face.

"I plan to."

"I'll drive you." He started for the door, then stopped when she didn't follow. "What's wrong?"

"I can get to the doctor on my own."

"How? By driving?"

"Yes—by driving."

He frowned. "And suppose you have another dizzy spell or black out while you're driving? What then? You could hurt yourself, the baby and God knows who else."

She hadn't thought of that, Regan conceded. Cole was right. She really had no business driving as long as she was having these dizzy spells. Still, she had no intention of going anywhere with Cole—not until she had a long conversation with her Aunt Liz and figured out exactly what she was going to do. "I'll get Amy to drive me or I'll take a taxi."

"I *said* I'd take you."

Refusing to be bullied, Regan sank down on the chair behind her desk. "I appreciate the offer. But I prefer going alone."

His lips thinned. Marching over to her, he planted both hands firmly on the desk's surface and leaned in so that she was forced to look at him. "Let's get something straight, princess. That baby you're carrying is mine. And I have no intention of letting you shut me out of any decisions or matters where my child is concerned. I have rights as the father, and I intend to exercise them."

The mention of his parental rights brought Regan's predicament slamming home. She didn't doubt for a second that Cole was telling her the truth. That he had been her sperm donor. But she had no intention of admitting as much to him. Not yet anyway. Oh, Aunt Liz, how could you have done this to me? What if Cole fights me for the baby? What if…?

Regan clamped down on the panic bubbling inside her and once again reminded herself that she wasn't the naive, love-struck girl Cole had married all those years ago. She was an independent, responsible woman now—a woman who refused to be intimidated by the likes of Cole Thornton. She shoved back her chair and stood. Squaring her shoulders, Regan tipped up her chin and said, "*If* this is in fact your baby that I'm carrying, then you and I will talk about your rights with our lawyers. But until I confirm that with my aunt, I suggest you back off."

"Go ahead and talk to Liz. But if I were you, princess, I'd start getting used to the idea of me being around. Because I intend to be a part of my child's life."

Marching over to the door, Regan held it open for him. "If Aunt Liz confirms your story, I'll have my lawyer get in touch with you."

He walked over to where she stood with her back ramrod straight, her hand on the doorknob. He stood so close to her, she could smell the spicy scent of his cologne. As he stared at her, a devilish glint came into his eyes. Slowly, he slid his gaze down the length of her, then back up again, and Regan's pulse began to stammer. When his eyes locked with hers again, his mouth twisted into that crooked smile that had made a seventeen-year-old girl fall head-over-heels in love. "Don't worry. Liz will confirm my story."

"We'll see."

His smile widened, giving her the full benefit of that killer smile. "One more thing, princess," he murmured softly, catching her chin and leaning in close.

"What?" she asked breathlessly, far too aware of his nearness and the feel of his fingers on her skin.

"Forget about having your lawyer call." He brushed his mouth against hers, a featherlike caress that sent tremors through her body, awakening memories and needs buried ages ago. When he lifted his head, he took her hand and pressed a card into her palm. "My cell phone number's on there. *You* call me."

But Regan didn't call—not that afternoon or the next. Nor did she respond to any of the messages he'd left at her office, her home or on her car phone. Caught somewhere between irritation and concern, Cole half-listened on his cell phone to the hotel operator as she read off a string of new phone messages to him. Apparently everyone wanted to speak with him—his assistant, his banker, his stockbroker. Even the luscious redhead he'd met in Paris last week who had somehow managed to track him down at the hotel in New Orleans. Everyone wanted to speak with him—except Regan.

As the hotel operator droned on, Cole paced the length of the veranda at the front of the St. Claire estate, where he'd spent the past two hours waiting for Regan. Leaning on the banister, he stared up at the sky. The sun had set long ago, leaving a slight nip in the air. A full moon lit up the heavens, and stars splattered across the skyline, shimmering like diamonds on beds of black velvet.

"That's the last of this batch, Mr. Thornton," the operator said.

"Um, thank you," Cole murmured, rubbing his weary

eyes. "Just leave those in my box at the front desk with the others. But if Ms. St. Claire should call—"

"We'll have her phone you on your cellular right away," the operator said, then read off the number he'd left the other half-dozen times he'd checked in with the hotel on the off chance that Regan had tried to reach him there. "Don't worry, sir. Everyone at the front desk's been alerted that you're expecting a call from Ms. St. Claire. The minute she calls, we'll be sure to have her contact you."

"Thanks," Cole muttered as he ended the call, chagrined that he'd obviously made a nuisance of himself. "Dammit, Regan. Where are you? And why in the devil haven't you called me?"

But he had a feeling he already knew the answer. It was the kiss. Kissing her had been a mistake. He still wasn't sure what had possessed him to kiss her in the first place. The blasted woman had reminded him of a spitting cat yesterday afternoon with her green eyes flashing, that stubborn chin of hers poking up in the air while she ordered him to back off. He'd only meant to ruffle her fur a bit. Instead he'd been the one to get ruffled. Hell, ruffled didn't come close to what that one kiss had done to him. A simple case of attraction had turned into full-blown lust and short-circuited his brain.

Dammit, he'd frightened her. Hell, he'd scared himself, he admitted. Because he'd wanted her with a fierceness that bordered on pain. And she'd known it, too. That was the reason she hadn't called him. He'd pushed her too hard, too fast—just as he had twelve years ago when he'd used her pregnancy to bind her to him in marriage. She hadn't been ready for marriage. He'd known it, but he'd pushed her anyway because he'd been afraid he would lose her. Thinking back to that time, to the mistakes that he'd made, Cole cursed his impatience and all that it had cost him. Regan had been so innocent—part girl, part woman and pure temptation. She'd been caught up in the flush of her first passion and too blinded to know the difference between lust and love. He, on the other hand, had been born old and was long past innocent. The four-year difference in their ages might as well have been forty. He had known from the time he was six years old what he wanted in life—to be rich, successful, respected—and he'd made up his mind to do whatever was necessary to make it happen. He'd allowed nothing and no one to deter him from the path he'd set for himself.

Until Regan.

He hadn't counted on her coming into his life…on him wanting her, needing her, loving her. She was everything he'd ever dreamed of in a mate. Only she had come into his life too soon—before he'd been able to make himself into *somebody,* before he'd had a right to love her, to expect her to love him. But he'd been selfish and loved her anyway. And for the short time that she'd been his, he had felt less alone. He'd almost believed that she truly loved him, that who and what he was didn't matter.

Of course, it had mattered. He grimaced as he reflected upon his self-delusions. Even now, the admission of his stupidity left a bitter taste in his mouth. How had he ever allowed himself to believe that a sharp mind, a strong back and ambition would wipe out the fact that he was the bastard son of a woman who cleaned houses for a living? He hadn't belonged in Regan's world of black-tie dinners, designer gowns and blue bloods. Just as she hadn't belonged in his world of two jobs, rundown apartments, and no time to hit the study books. So he'd pushed her. And in the end, his impatience had cost him not only Regan, but the life of his unborn child.

The hollow ache that always came with thoughts of the baby daughter who had died before she'd ever had a chance to live threatened to claim him now. Dwelling on the past was the last thing he needed. He couldn't change the past, Cole reminded himself. He needed to think of the future, of the new baby growing inside Regan.

His baby. Regardless of the circumstances, they had conceived another child together, which meant he and Regan were once again a part of each other's lives. Once again, Regan and their unborn baby were his responsibilities. And, unlike his own father, *he* intended to live up to his responsibilities—even if it meant fighting Regan to do it. No child of his was going to be subjected to taunts and whispers, made to feel his or her birth had been a mistake. His child was never going to wonder who daddy was because his child was going to have his last name. A fact which he intended to make clear to Regan—just as soon as she got home.

If she got home. Cole stared at the cell phone, willed the thing to ring. It remained silent instead. Impatient, he flipped the phone open and started to punch in Liz's number again. Just as quickly he slapped the thing shut. If Liz had heard from Regan, she would have called him—especially after he'd taken his well-meaning friend to task for meddling in his and Regan's lives. Besides, Liz had said that when Regan had stormed out of the clinic four hours ago, she'd been royally miffed with her aunt and had claimed that she needed to think about what she was going to do.

So where the devil did you go to do your thinking, princess?

A late March wind, heavy with the scent of night jasmine, whistled through moss-draped oak trees that stood along the property that had been in Regan's family since the turn of the century. The familiar scents of New Orleans brought back a rush of memories. Memories of the tiny, dank apartments where he had lived with his mother as a boy, places that had been sweltering hot in the summer and freezing cold in the winter. Other memories washed over him like scenes in a kaleidoscope—memories of his mother working, struggling to make ends meet by scrubbing floors in other people's homes until her hands were worn and wrinkled. Unable to stop the flood of memories, he squeezed his eyes shut as the scenes tumbled behind his closed lids. His mother serving the fancy guests at parties in the beautiful homes. His mother shuffling him off to a corner in a kitchen and telling him to be a good boy while she worked. Him sneaking peeks at the party guests and wanting to join the other kids there. Him wishing he could be like those other kids, wishing that he belonged.

Cole opened his eyes and drew in a cleansing breath. Bracing his back against one of the home's stately columns, he listened to the tinkling of a wind chime somewhere. The musical sound triggered another memory—a memory of other nights like this one—nights when, as a youth, he'd wandered through the dark, narrow streets of the French Quarter, lured by the soulful music and sultry scents, the ghostly tales of pirates and voodoo, the promises of sex and sin that lurked on every corner. He recalled how quickly one turn down a wrong street could prove not only dangerous, but deadly. Suddenly fear knotted like a fist in Cole's stomach. How many times had Regan taken off to roam the French Quarter streets when she'd wanted to be alone to mull over a problem or brood about an argument with her father?

What if Regan had gone walking in the French Quarter tonight to think?

Bile rose in Cole's throat at the thought. She knew the area like the back of her hand, the places to avoid, the areas no woman or man should ever venture alone, Cole told himself.

But what if she had another dizzy spell? Or if, in her distressed state, she wandered down one of those wrong streets?

Cole's heart slammed against his ribs, and he took off across the veranda at a run. "Damn! Damn! Damn!" He should have insisted on going with her. She and the baby were his responsibilities now. If anything had happened to her or the baby—

Cole shut off the thought, refused to even give credence to the notion that something could have happened to her.

Still, he raced down the stairs, taking them two at a time. His feet had barely cleared the last step when the black iron gates fronting the property's entrance swung open, and Regan's white BMW came cruising up the long driveway.

Relief flooded through Cole, making his heart kick. Remembering past mistakes, Cole forced himself to stay put, not to rush out to meet her and demand an explanation of where she had been. It took Regan no more than a few minutes to park the car and maneuver the path to the house, but to Cole it seemed an eternity. An eternity in which he jammed his hands into his pockets and dug deeply inside himself for patience while every instinct demanded he snag her close, run his hands over her and assure himself she was unharmed.

"Cole," she said, her voice strained, her expression wary. "I didn't expect to see you here."

From the expression on her face, he knew that she hadn't *wanted* to see him here. The realization smarted more than Cole had thought possible, but he handled it as he had so many others in his life—by focusing on his goal. And his goal at the moment was the baby. "I didn't hear from you," he said, taking care to keep any accusation out of his tone. "When I couldn't reach you by phone, I came here. Since you weren't home, I decided to wait." He saw no point in telling her that he'd been waiting for more than two hours, that he'd called everyone he could think of, searching for her, and that he'd been about to start tearing the city apart to find her.

"Looks like you didn't have any trouble getting past the security gates."

"No."

She arched her brow in that imperious way that had amused him so often years ago. "I was led to believe my security system was top of the line and practically burglar-proof. Obviously, that's not true."

Cole curved his mouth into a grin. "There's nothing

wrong with your system, princess. It's actually among the best available. But one of the companies I own designs computer software for home security systems. It just so happens that your security firm uses my company's software. Since I designed the program, I also know how to override the codes.''

"How convenient for you."

"Yes. It is, isn't it?"

A phone rang inside the house. "I'm afraid you'll have to excuse me. That's probably my Aunt Liz," Regan said, moving past him to head up the stairs. As she did so, Cole caught a whiff of her perfume. It was the same brand she'd worn when he'd first met her—a special blend that reminded him of honeysuckle. The fragrance immediately hurled him back to another time—to an evening spent making love with Regan and of waking the next morning to the scent of honeysuckle on his sheets. Cole sucked in a breath, fought the swift rush of desire that hit him and the sudden tightness in his chest. Hormones again, he told himself. Nothing more. He certainly wasn't dumb enough to let himself fall under the woman's spell a second time. She'd cured him of any romantic notions he'd had about love the first time he'd tangled with her. Baby or no baby, it wasn't a lesson that he intended to forget.

Cole hesitated in front of the doors of the mansion. He couldn't help thinking back to the very first time the butler had opened those doors for him. He'd felt like a mongrel with muddy feet. Shaking off the memory, he stepped inside the grand foyer entrance. The place was every bit as cold and imposing as he remembered, Cole thought. He swept his gaze over the high ceilings, the marble floors and silk wall coverings that echoed refinement and wealth handed down through generations. And despite the fact that he was now a millionaire a hundred times over, standing beneath the crystal chandelier amidst the elegance, he still felt like a mongrel who didn't belong here.

"Yes, Aunt Liz, I'm okay. I'm sorry you were worried. I know he has. He's here now," Regan's voice carried from the opposite end of the foyer, where she stood with her back to him as she spoke into the telephone receiver. "No, I haven't decided yet. Yes, I'll call you later and let you know. I love you, too."

When she hung up the phone and turned around, Cole got a good look at Regan for the first time since he'd left her. Yesterday, all the old resentments that had begun to eat at him disappeared the minute he saw her face. In the moon-light and with the trees shading her face, he hadn't been able to see her clearly. From her reaction to his presence, he had assumed she was okay. But now...now he could see that she was far from okay. She didn't have a lick of color in her cheeks. Faint shadows marred the delicate skin beneath her eyes. And despite her regal posture, she looked as though a strong wind would knock her right off her feet. A surge of warmth and tenderness, two emotions he hadn't associated with Regan for years, pumped through his system. The fact that he felt those emotions for her now grated. "What's wrong?"

She arched her brow. "You mean aside from the mess we find ourselves in?"

He narrowed his eyes, told himself he wasn't hurt that she considered their situation to be a mess. "I mean you look like hell."

"Gee, thanks. That's just what every pregnant woman wants to hear."

Cole swore, dragged in a breath. "What I meant was you don't look well. You look...exhausted."

"I'm fine."

"Did you eat anything? I heard that pregnant women need to eat lots of small meals, and that—"

"I'm fine, Cole," she insisted, her voice tight, strained. "I'm just tired. And to be honest, I'm not up to playing

word games tonight. You already know that I saw Aunt Liz
and that she…she confirmed your story.''

"My story?'' Cole repeated, irritated that she seemed to
find it so difficult to say that he was the father of the child
she carried. He followed her into the living room.

"That you were the sperm donor for my baby.''

"Our baby,'' he corrected and had the satisfaction of seeing those green eyes flash with annoyance. But his satisfaction was short-lived and made him feel small because it was
obvious she was dead on her feet. "Sit down—before you
fall down.''

She hesitated for all of two seconds, then sank to the
couch. She looked so fragile and lost sitting there. Something inside Cole unfurled, making him want to draw her
into his arms and promise her everything would be all right.
Instead, he claimed the chair across from her. Several heart-
beats passed in an awkward silence. Then, sighing, Cole
leaned forward and said, "I owe you an apology. I honestly
thought Liz had told you that she'd approached me about
being a sperm donor for you.''

"I know. She told me what happened. She also told me
that you had apparently changed your mind.'' Regan stared
down at her hands as though she hoped to find the answers
she sought there. "I'm sorry, too. If I'd had any idea…''

Regan didn't finish. But then, she didn't need to, because
he knew he'd been right. He *was* the last man she'd have
chosen to have a child with.

"I know Aunt Liz meant well. But she's put us both in
an impossible situation.''

"Awkward maybe, but not impossible,'' Cole offered,
wanting to ease some of the tension. "There are options
available to us. Several in fact.'' But there was only one
option he could live with. And as much as Regan wouldn't
like it, he had no intention of settling for anything less than
the course he'd decided upon already.

Her head snapped up. "I'm going to have this baby.''

"Do you honestly believe I would suggest you not have it?" He bit back the sharp jab that she might think such a thing of him. "Regardless of how this pregnancy came about, I want this baby."

"The only question is how we're going to deal with custody."

Her eyes slapped to his, narrowed. "This is *my* baby, Cole. *Mine.* I'd already planned on being a single mother. I have no intention of shuttling my child back and forth between me and its father. That's not what I want for my baby."

"*Our* baby," he corrected her again. "And I agree. I don't want our child shuttled back and forth between us either."

Hesitating, she curled her fingers into her skirt. "Does that mean you…that you would be willing to relinquish your rights and let me raise the baby?"

Her words hit him like blows. Gritting his teeth, Cole worked to keep his emotions in check. After all, it wasn't the first time he hadn't been found good enough, he reminded himself. In her eyes for a child to have no father would probably be preferable than to have him as one. But like it or not, it was his baby she was carrying, and he had no intention of walking away from his responsibilities. He forced his lips into a smile. "Sorry to disappoint you, princess, but that's not what I had in mind."

"But you agreed that you didn't want our baby to be shuttled back and forth between us."

"I don't," he assured her. "I think a child belongs with both of its parents."

"But that's not possible."

"Sure it is. All we have to do is get married."

Three

——

"**M**arried?" Regan sputtered, grateful to be sitting because suddenly the oxygen flow to her brain seemed in short supply. Surely she had misunderstood him. "You can't mean that the two of us...that you and I...that we should marry each other?"

"That is usually how it works," Cole said dryly, the line of his jaw so rigid it could have been chiseled in steel. "As I recall, it's a fairly simple procedure. We stand up before a justice of the peace or a minister and promise to love, honor and cherish each other. After that we—"

"I remember how it's done," she snapped, temper and nerves cutting through her shock. Did he really think she had forgotten exchanging vows with him twelve years ago? That she would ever forget that he had once pledged to love her forever? Emotions swirled inside her. Her throat grew tighter by the second. Darn it, not now. She blinked back the tears already blurring her vision and rued her hair-trigger emotions since becoming pregnant. The last thing she wanted to do was cry in front of Cole. But given the bomb-shells he had dropped on her—first that he was her baby's father and now his cold offer of marriage—she was very much afraid she was going to start blubbering any second. Shoving to her feet, she hurried across the room to stand before the sweep of windows that overlooked the gardens. She took a deep breath and attempted to regain some sem-blance of composure while she stared at row after row of azaleas, their lush blooms of pink and white illuminated by the discreetly placed lights. Usually just looking at the gar-den soothed her. But now, even the beauty of nature's rebirth failed to stop Cole's emotionless proposal from ringing in her ears. She couldn't help but remember the last time he had proposed to her—the tender way he had looked at her as he held her in his arms and told her that he loved her.

"Then you'll also remember that the whole deal is rela-tively quick and painless. If we apply for a marriage license tomorrow, we should be able to get married by the end of the week."

Regan whipped around. Cole stood so close his powerful shoulders narrowed her field of vision to the expanse of white shirt covering his impressive chest. The scent of spice and male filled her nostrils. She could see the pulse that beat in his neck, the new beard growth that created five-o'clock shadows along his cheeks. Swallowing, she moved her gaze upward, and her pulse scattered at the intensity of the silver eyes trained on her mouth. Suddenly she felt the way she had at seventeen—nervous and excited by the desire re-flected in those eyes—a part of her wanting him to kiss her, a part of her afraid that he would.

"I can take care of whatever arrangements are necessary. All you have to do is show up."

The cut-and-dry offer hit Regan like a splash of cold water in the face. "You can't possibly be serious," she tossed back, furious with herself for nearly falling under Cole's seductive spell again.

"Believe me. I've never been more serious about anything in my life. We should get married. And the sooner, the better."

If his solemn tone hadn't convinced her he was serious, the cold, hard gleam in his eyes certainly had. Cole *was* serious. He actually expected her to marry him again. She pressed a fist to her breast to ease this new dent he'd put in her heart. There had been a time when she had dreamed, even prayed for them to find their way back to each other. But not like this. Never like this. The thought of marrying Cole now—simply for the sake of the baby—set off a fresh wave of pain inside her. "Thanks, but I think I'll pass."

"You'll pass?" he repeated as though he couldn't believe she'd turned him down.

"That's right."

His mouth hardened. "In case it's slipped your mind, princess, I'm a very wealthy man now. There are any number of women who would consider themselves lucky to become Mrs. Cole Thornton."

"Then I suggest you ask one of them to marry you."

Anger flashed in his eyes. He moved even closer until she could feel the rush of his breath on her face, the heat from his body. "*You're* the one who happens to be carrying my child."

"Which is the same reason we got married the last time." At least it was the reason he had married her, Regan admitted. "It didn't work out then, and I can't see it working out now."

"Things are different now," he told her, his voice softening.

"Are they?" she whispered, wanting to believe him.

"Yes." He brushed his thumb along her cheek. "This time I can take care of you and our child."

"I don't need to be taken care of," she informed him, turning away from his touch and chiding herself for being disappointed. "And I can take care of my baby."

"That child you're carrying is mine, too. He or she deserves to be brought up in a home with both parents."

"You know it's not that simple," she insisted.

"It *is* simple. We're going to have a baby. I'm suggesting we do the right thing by getting married. That's all. Don't make it more complicated than it is."

But it was complicated. Terribly complicated. She hugged her arms around herself. And the biggest complication of all was that she still had feelings for Cole while he…he had none for her. "It would never work."

"Why not?"

"For lots of reasons."

"Name one."

Because you don't love me, she wanted to say. Instead she replied, "For starters, we're practically strangers."

His hands closed over her shoulders, and Cole turned her to face him. Slowly, oh so slowly, he skimmed his gaze over her in a visual caress that had Regan's blood spinning. When his eyes met hers, he murmured, "We're hardly strangers, princess."

Regan swallowed hard, tried to shut off the stirring inside her. "You know what I mean. We don't know each other anymore."

"Are you sure?" He moved in close again, until his body was only a breath away from hers. "I know you're very sensitive here," he said, tucking a strand of hair behind her ear, then tracing the shell of her ear with his fingertip.

Regan's heart pumped frantically as his clever finger moved slowly from her ear to her neck, leaving a trail of fire along her skin and desire curling in her belly.

Cole lowered his head, bringing his mouth just shy of hers. "And I know that when I kiss you," he whispered, his breath teasing her lips while he smoothed a finger along her neck. "I know that the pulse here beats like a hummingbird's wings."

Her eyes fluttered closed, and Regan braced herself for

the gentle brush of Cole's lips against hers. He took her mouth instead. There was nothing soft or sweet or gentle about this kiss. It was hot, hungry, demanding—like the man. His fingers speared through her hair, anchored themselves at her nape. "Open for me, princess," he commanded, his voice hoarse with a need that should have frightened her, but excited her instead.

Desire spun through Regan's blood, clouded her senses. She parted her lips. Cole groaned, and Regan shuddered as he claimed her mouth again and again—thrusting his tongue inside to dance and duel with her own. He slid his hands down her back, cupped her bottom, drew her against him. His arousal pressed against her belly, hot and heavy, and the feel of him sent a thrill of excitement, of anticipation through Regan. She wanted him, she admitted. Fisting her hands in his shirt, she held on as heat streaked through her like lightning.

Nothing had changed, Regan conceded, as she succumbed to the power of Cole's kiss. It had always been like this between them—this instant fire, this all-consuming need that sparked with little more than a look, the most innocent touch. This urgent desire that blazed white-hot and out of control until they were both naked and their bodies joined as one, as man and woman were meant to be. If she married Cole, it could be that way again, Regan reasoned. Deep in her heart she knew she still loved him, that she had never stopped loving him. And Cole...

Regan sobered. Cole didn't love her. He hadn't even mentioned the word *love*.

As though he sensed her withdrawal, Cole lifted his head. When she looked into his eyes, she caught the flare of victory, and desire died as quickly as it had sprung to life, leaving a sick, hollow ache in its place. She pushed at Cole's shoulders, and he released her at once. What a silly, romantic fool she was, she admitted, burning with humiliation at how close she had come to saying yes to him. She moved past him to the bar, where she snagged a bottle of mineral water from the mini-fridge.

How could she have forgotten how determined Cole could be? Nothing kept him from reaching his goals. And this time the goal he'd set for himself was to marry her for their baby's sake. If reasoning didn't work, he certainly wasn't above seducing her to make sure he got what he wanted.

Hands trembling, Regan poured water into a glass and drank deeply, trying to drown the last of the fantasies his kisses had ignited.

"What's wrong?"

She clenched her fingers around the glass, resisted the urge to slap it down on the bar. "Nothing," she said in a voice her charm-school teacher would have been proud of since it sounded so calm and refined. She hiked up her chin. "Except that you don't know me quite as well as you think you do. I'm not a naive girl anymore. And despite your skill as a lover, I can't be so easily seduced this time."

A muscle twitched in his jaw. His eyes took on the color of flint. "Is that how it was between us, princess? You were just an innocent girl and I seduced you?"

Shame sent heat shooting up her cheeks. "No," she admitted honestly. If anything, she had been the one to seduce him. She'd known almost from the moment she'd first seen him that Cole was the man she wanted to spend her life with. Falling in love with him hadn't been an option for her. She'd loved him from the start, and when he'd insisted they couldn't be together, she had set out to make him change his mind. And she'd succeeded. "I shouldn't have said that. We both know that we became lovers because I wanted you."

"True. But I didn't exactly fight you off, did I? And I was the one responsible for getting you pregnant."

Regan shook her head. "It's a little late for either one of us to be slinging arrows of blame. The past doesn't matter now. It would be better if we just forget it."

"That's going to be a bit difficult, don't you think? I mean seeing how we're right back where we were twelve years ago. You're pregnant, and I'm the guy responsible."

"It's not the same, and you know it."

"What I know is that the baby you're carrying is mine. Which makes you and the baby my responsibilities."

Regan wanted to scream. "I am *not* your responsibility, and I'd appreciate it if you'd quit saying I was."

Cole uncurled her fingers from around the glass and captured both of her hands in his. His expression softened. "You're going to be the mother of my child. After…after we lost our little girl, I'd pretty much decided I was never going to have children. I didn't want to risk that kind of hurt, to feel I'd failed so badly, ever again. But when I found out about this baby…" He paused. "When I found out about this baby, I knew I wanted another chance to be a father. Give me that chance, princess. Marry me."

There was such a wealth of loneliness in his voice, in his eyes. It tugged at Regan's heart, reminded her of the man she had fallen in love with—the loner who hadn't believed he deserved to be loved, the young Cole who hadn't trusted that anyone could love him. Despite all his success, Cole seemed somehow even more alone now than he had been. She wanted to wrap her arms around him. Instinctively, she knew to do so would be a mistake.

Cole desired her. It was there in his eyes, in the hunger of his kiss. And while he might welcome her passion, he would never welcome her comfort or her love. Reminding herself of that fact, Regan managed to ease her fingers free. "We tried marriage, and it ended up being a major bust despite the fact that we…that I loved you. For us to marry again now would never work."

"We could make it work…for the baby's sake."

Regan shook her head. "It takes more than sharing a child to make a marriage work."

"We have more," he told her. "The chemistry is still there between us."

When she started to object, Cole stroked her bottom lip with his thumb. "Don't bother denying it, princess. All I have to do is look at you, and I want you. And I know it's the same way for you."

Regan flushed because it was true. "You're talking about sex. Not love."

"From what I've seen, sex is a hell of a lot more honest than love. At least with sex there are no illusions, no disappointments." He tipped her chin up so that she was forced to meet his eyes. "We tried love once, and it didn't work. The way I see it, we have a better shot at making marriage work between us this time because we wouldn't be confusing sex with love."

Regan swallowed hard, to keep back the tears pricking behind her eyes at his remark. "And the way I see it, you're a man who's forgotten how to dream."

His jaw tightened. "I don't see any point in wasting time on dreams. I decide what I want and do what I have to in order to get it."

"Is that what you're doing now, Cole? Asking me to marry you in order to get what you want—which in this case is our baby?"

"I'm asking you to marry me because it's the right thing to do. I want to take care of you and be a real father to our child."

His words were another swipe at Regan's heart. "Whether or not you're a father to this baby is up to you. I can't stop you from being a part of his or her life. I wouldn't even try. But you'll have to do it without marrying me." Tears now only a breath away began to swim in her eyes, and Regan knew she wasn't going to be able to hold them back much longer. "Now, if you'll excuse me. I've had a long day, and I'm very tired."

"But—"

"I'd like you to leave, Cole. Now."

"Regan—"

"Just go," she cried out. "Please."

Something in her face must have told him she was near the end of her rope, because he didn't press her further. He turned and started out the room, only to pause at the door. "This discussion isn't over, princess. Get some rest, and we'll talk again in the morning."

But he didn't talk to Regan again in the morning, or in the afternoon, or during any of the other dozen times he had attempted to reach her. The infuriating woman had left town—a maneuver which Cole hadn't anticipated. Of course, neither her aunt nor her staff claimed to know where she had gone on this impromptu vacation, or when she would be returning.

Fortunately, he had the money to hire someone to find the answers for him, Cole reasoned several days later as he sat across the table in his hotel suite from Mac Mackenzie, a former government agent who operated a string of investigative agencies.

"She's in South Carolina," Mackenzie informed him. "Staying at a place owned by a friend of hers from college—a sorority sister by the name of Maggie Carmichael."

Before he could stop himself, Cole began firing questions at the other man. "Is she all right? She's not sick, is she? And this Maggie person, is she staying with her in case something goes wrong?" Only now was he able to admit just how worried he had been about Regan. He'd spent the better part of the last three days with images of Regan running through his head—of her getting sick as she had that afternoon at the jewelry store, of her having another one of those dizzy spells, of her looking so fragile and weak. The worst of the lot had been while he had lain awake at night in bed, because that's when he kept imagining Regan alone somewhere, in pain and suffering a miscarriage as she had the last time. And just like the last time, he wouldn't be there to help her.

"She seemed fine to me, but here take a look for yourself." The detective removed several photos from a large manilla envelope and shoved them across the table toward Cole. Obviously taken with a telephoto lens, the texture was grainy, but there was no mistaking the woman. It was Regan. There were at least a dozen shots—Regan walking along the beach, Regan wading at the water's edge, Regan sitting in the sand and hugging her knees while the surf danced over her bare toes. Though her expression was solemn, she looked healthy. And impossibly sad.

"She's alone, and my guess is she wants it that way. She hasn't been into town at all. She has the groceries delivered. And the only place she goes when she leaves the house is to the beach, and then she only goes when no one else is around. The rest of the time she sits out on the deck reading or just gazing out at the water."

No surprises there, Cole conceded. Happy or sad, Regan had always been drawn to the water. Their honeymoon, brief as it was, had been spent at a cheap motel on a beach along the Mississippi Gulf Coast because she'd wanted to be able to hear the sound of the surf whenever they left the room. He traced a finger over the face in the pictures, remembering the passionate and spirited girl/woman she'd been, the independent woman she'd become—the woman who had his child growing inside her once again. The need to protect her and the baby was so powerful it overwhelmed him. He wanted to go to her, to see with his own eyes that she was safe. But to do so would be a mistake, Cole admitted, because Regan would turn him away. Yet he couldn't sit here and do nothing. He had failed once before to keep her and their child safe when he hadn't stopped Regan from leaving him. He didn't want to fail again now.

He wouldn't fail, Cole promised himself. Regan and the baby were his responsibilities. Whether she liked it or not, he would honor those responsibilities. "Thanks, Mac. You've done a good job. I appreciate it."

"Glad to be of service," Mackenzie replied. He stood, obviously taking Cole's comment as his cue that their discussion was over.

Cole rose. "I'd like for you to continue to keep an eye on her for me."

"No problem. I've got one of my operatives keeping her under surveillance while I'm here. I'll have him stay on the job until I can get back."

Cole nodded, pleased by the man's thoroughness. "In the meantime, if you're interested, I have another job for you."

"What do you need?"

"Anything and everything you can get me on a local jewelry store called Exclusives," Cole advised him, deciding to check out the suspicion that had nagged at him since he'd been at Regan's store. The place had been nearly empty and seemed to employ only a skeleton staff—not at all the bustle of activity that it had been years ago. The fact that there had been no staff waiting at the house for her when he'd arrived had also seemed odd, but he'd simply attributed it to Regan downsizing since her father's death. At the time he hadn't been thinking clearly or he might have suspected sooner that there could be another reason for the downsizing. But he was thinking clearly now. After discussing the scope of what he wanted with the detective, he saw the other man to the door. "And, Mac?"

"Yes?" the detective turned, his shrewd brown gaze meeting Cole's.

"I want to be notified the minute she leaves South Carolina. Day or night, it doesn't matter when. Just make sure I get the call."

The call came late the following week. By the time Cole had been notified that Regan's plane had landed at the airport in New Orleans, he was ready. Seated on the swing of the veranda at the stuffy museum she called home, he rubbed the tense muscles at the base of his neck. He'd negotiated multimillion-dollar business ventures with a lot less trepidation than this. Proposing marriage, even to a woman who had refused him once, should not have acid churning in his stomach and his nerves wound up tighter than a spring. But it did, he admitted in disgust. The bottom line was he'd always had a weakness where Regan was concerned—a fact that time and success hadn't altered. If anything, the situation was worse now because if she turned down his offer of marriage again, he would have no choice but to play his ace. And instead of a marriage proposal he'd present her with a marriage bargain—one that she would be forced to accept.

Cole's mouth twisted with distaste over the lengths he was prepared to go to ensure his child be born legitimate. He didn't much like himself for being so ruthless. But he would see it through if needed. He sighed, hating the idea of backing Regan into a corner with threats. It would be so much simpler for both of them if she just agreed to marry him.

Simpler and more enjoyable, Cole admitted, recalling the taste and feel of Regan in his arms ten days ago. She'd been so sweet and passionate when he'd kissed her. For a short time, honoring his responsibilities had been the last thing on his mind. He'd been rock-hard in an instant and as eager as an untried teenager to make love to her. And he was growing aroused all over again just thinking about her, Cole realized.

He bit back a groan of frustration, knowing he didn't have a prayer of satisfying that desire anytime soon. And maybe never if she discovered what he had done. Leaning back against the porch swing, he stared up at an ebony sky dusted with stars, but his thoughts remained on Regan. Would she end up hating him when she found out the truth? Probably, he conceded. He regretted that. But what choice did he have? She and the baby were his responsibilities.

Not that she would see it that way. She wouldn't. Just as she wouldn't understand his need to protect her and the baby. But then, why should she? Growing up in a tight-knit community where acceptance went hand-in-hand with a good family name and money, Regan didn't know what it would be like to find herself and her child neither accepted nor welcomed. But he knew. Just as he knew how the doors now open to her would suddenly close, the invitations would stop and the elite clientele she depended on would steer clear of her jewelry store once the word spread that she was pregnant and had no husband. The world might have just entered a new millennium, but in the social circles of the New Orleans where Regan lived, it could just as easily be Victorian England. She would become a social outcast. Without his name to protect her, even her so-called friends would abandon her. And as bad as it would be for Regan, for their baby it would be even worse.

Fury ripped through Cole at the mere thought of Regan and their baby being subjected to the sly whispers and knowing looks, to the cruelties he had endured growing up here. He knew all too well how it felt to be considered not good enough. Hell, hadn't Philip St. Claire told him as much? Tossed his illegitimacy back in his teeth?

Scrubbing a hand down his face, Cole struggled to get a grip on his emotions. He thought about the results of Mackenzie's investigation. Whether he'd done the right thing or not no longer mattered, because now it was too late to turn back. He'd already set things in motion. Honor bound him to do whatever was necessary to protect Regan and the baby. And the only way to make good on that commitment was to marry Regan.

But making good on his commitment was not going to be easy, Cole concluded, when Regan arrived ten minutes later and barely paused at the sight of him waiting on her veranda.

He jogged down the stairs to meet her. The moon slanted over her face like the deft strokes of an artist's brush, accentuating her high cheekbones, her too-full mouth, her long slender neck. Streaks of white gold shot through the blonde hair that had been left unbound and fell nearly to her waist. Desire that had been gnawing at him since he'd kissed her two weeks ago ripped into him now with greedy claws. It was just one more thing that hadn't changed. He itched to claim that ripe mouth of hers now, to feed the fierce hunger that had kept him awake nights thinking of her and wanting her, to run his hands over every inch of that silken skin and assure himself that she was truly all right. "Welcome home, princess."

"Hello, Cole," she replied politely, tempting him to haul her into his arms and wipe that cool look from her eyes.

To prevent himself from doing just that, he reached for the small suitcase she held. "You don't seem surprised to see me," he said, motioning for her to precede him up the stairs.

She shrugged. "I had a hunch you'd be waiting for me."

"Looks like your hunch was right." Despite his glib manner, uneasiness inched down Cole's spine. While he was pleased she appeared less stressed, he couldn't shake the feeling that more than her vacation was responsible for this newfound calmness.

"Actually it was more than a hunch," she admitted. "Aunt Liz told me you were still in town. It wasn't difficult to figure out why you'd suddenly decide to spend so much time in a place you've managed to avoid for more than a decade."

"Maybe there was never a reason for me to come back—until now."

"Because of my baby."

"Because of *our* baby," he amended.

She slid the key into the lock. Hesitating, she glanced up at him. "I don't suppose I can convince you to put off this discussion until tomorrow?"

He lifted a lock of her silky blond hair, curved it around his index finger. "You're welcome to try to convince me," he told her, keeping his voice deliberately soft. She slapped his hand away, then sighed. "I was really looking forward to a nice, long soak in the tub—not arguing with you."

"You can still have that soak and we can skip the arguing," he informed her. "All you have to do is set a wedding date."

Green fire flashed in her eyes. "There isn't going to be a wedding," she told him, then whirled around and entered the house.

Once again, the inkling that Regan was up to something stirred in Cole's gut as he followed her inside. "Where would you like me to put this?" Cole asked, indicating the suitcase he still held.

"By the door is fine." She moved over to the bar and retrieved a bottle of water from the mini-fridge. "Since you're obviously not going to leave until we hash this out, would you like something to drink? I have wine, soda and I think there's a bottle of that Scotch you used to like."

"Scotch is fine," Cole replied.

"Still drink it on the rocks?"

Cole nodded, surprised and pleased that she remembered. She splashed the liquor over ice, and as she did so, he caught the slightest tremor in her fingers. The lady wasn't nearly as calm as she pretended to be, he realized. When she walked over to him and held out the glass, Cole reached for it, wrapped his fingers around hers. "Enough stalling, princess. You've had ten days to get used to the idea. So I'm asking you again. Will you marry me?"

"I can't."

"Can't? Or won't?"

"Won't," she replied, tugging her fingers free and sending Scotch sloshing over the rim of the glass and onto his hand. She took a step back. "I understand how you feel about the baby having your name, Cole. But getting married isn't the answer." A breath shuddered through her and then she continued, "I've talked to my attorney. She's drawing up the necessary paperwork for me to petition the court for primary custody of the baby when it's born. I've instructed her to make sure there are provisions included covering your visitation rights, and I'll make sure your name is listed on the birth certificate as the father.''

"That's very generous of you," he said, even though her tidy rejection left a bitter taste in his mouth. He saw no point in telling her that he'd already had similar documents drawn up a week ago, hoping they would prove enough of a weapon to get her to agree to this marriage.

"I would never deny you your rights as a father, Cole. But I'm also not going to compound one mistake by making another." Her speech evidently finished, she sliced him a glance. "I'm trying to be fair about this."

"I know you are," he conceded, already regretting what he was about to do. "But I'm afraid your offer isn't good enough."

She blinked. "Well, I'm sorry you feel that way, but it's the best I can do."

"Then let me make you another offer, princess," he said, knowing he was ten times the shark people had accused him of being for doing this to her. "Either you agree to marry me, or I'll call the mortgage on Exclusives."

"But the bank—"

"Sold it to me last week—along with a few others in a package deal."

All color drained from Regan's cheeks. "I don't have that kind of money."

A fact which he already knew and had counted on. The mortgage had been a hefty one that her father had taken out years ago to fund a failed expansion to the suburbs. Not quite the businessman he believed himself to be, Philip St. Claire had never got around to paying anything toward the principal. As a result, not only were Exclusives' inventory and equipment in hock, but so were all of the store's receivables and a substantial chunk of future business as well. Granted, Cole had scooped up the loan initially to ease Regan's stress level during the pregnancy—especially after a long chat with Liz that revealed her concerns about the pressure her niece was under and how it might adversely affect both her and the baby. He had never intended Regan to know. It would be a sort of silent wedding gift to her. But then, he hadn't expected Regan to dig in her heels and refuse to marry him either.

"Then I guess I'll just have to shut down the store and begin selling off the assets to recover my losses."

"You can't do that!"

"Trust me. I can do it, and I will—unless you agree to marry me," he lied, knowing full well he would never do such a thing to her.

"You really are a bastard," she snapped, the words an angry hiss.

"I've never denied it," Cole replied easily, but hearing her call him one smarted more than he'd expected. "So, what's it going to be, princess? Do I shut down the store, or do we get married?"

Four

Fury ripped through Regan. "You'd actually do that? Stoop to blackmail?"

"I'll do whatever I have to to make sure my child doesn't get labeled a bastard like his father."

His response took the sting out of her anger as nothing else possibly could, and left Regan filled with shame. How could she have allowed temper and frustration to cause her to resort to name-calling? And of all the colorful terms she could have used, why had she chosen the one guaranteed to cause him the most pain? Appalled by her behavior, she said, "Cole, just now when I...I didn't really mean..." Regan whooshed out a breath. "What I'm trying to say is that I'm sorry."

"Why?" he asked, his smile cold, cruel. "After all, it's the truth. I am a bastard, and nothing I do can ever change that fact. But I can make sure that my child isn't born a bastard, too."

Despite his glib reply, Regan saw the hurt beneath his

tough-as-nails demeanor. She'd never given his past too much thought when they'd been together because Cole had been so firmly focused on the future, not on looking back. Only now did she suspect how deep the scars were that he carried inside. But scars or not, it didn't make what he was doing right. "Listen, I know things weren't easy for you growing up. But times have changed. Things are different now. People aren't as narrow-minded as they were when you were a child. Just because we aren't married doesn't mean our baby is going to be branded with ugly names the way you were."

"If you believe things have changed that much, princess, I've got some swampland I'll sell you. You know as well as I do that the people in this city are caught in their own little time warp where a man's pedigree is every bit as important as his bank balance. If you think it won't matter to that ritzy crowd of yours that Ms. Regan St. Claire of the New Orleans St. Claires is pregnant and has no husband, you had better think again. Because it will matter."

"Then that's their problem," Regan tossed back. But deep down inside she knew Cole was right. New Orleans and the people who called the place home were indeed a breed unto themselves and still held fast to the moral conventions of another era. She'd known that when she had decided to try to have a child, but had gone ahead with her plan anyway. She didn't need anyone's approval, other than perhaps her Aunt Liz's, and she certainly didn't intend to marry Cole simply to satisfy someone else's antiquated idea of what was proper. "I don't care what anyone else thinks. It's none of their business what I do."

"Spoken like a true princess," Cole mocked. "Of course, *you* have never had to explain to anyone why you don't know who your father is."

"It wouldn't be like that. Our baby would know you're its father."

"And you think that will be enough?"

Regan's mouth thinned, but she remained silent, refusing to allow Cole to goad her into an argument.

"Tell me, princess. When our child realizes that mommy and daddy don't live together like most families, how do you plan to explain why? Do you think he or she is going to appreciate hearing that mommy's biological clock was ticking, but since she didn't want to be bothered with a husband, she just decided to get pregnant by an anonymous sperm donor?"

"It wasn't like that and you know it. I want this baby. That's why I was willing to use a sperm donor," she countered, her temper sparking at the unfairness of his accusation. "But what's your excuse, Cole? How do you explain agreeing to be the sperm donor?"

He eased a step closer, fastened his gaze on her mouth. When he lifted his hand and drew a finger down her cheek, a shiver of awareness skipped down Regan's spine. Heat curled low in her belly, and she ached to lift her mouth and touch it against his. But she refused to give in to that need, and waited for him to answer the question that had nagged at her for more than a week, the question that had given birth to a tiny bloom of hope in her heart that maybe Cole still cared for her. "Why, Cole? Why would you agree to father my child?"

"Liz convinced me I should have someone to carry on the Thornton name, someone to leave my fortune to. At the time it sounded like a good idea."

While she knew how persuasive her aunt could be, Cole was not a man who allowed himself to be persuaded into doing anything he didn't want to do. "But why me?" Regan persisted. "Why choose me to be the mother of your child?"

He was silent for so long, Regan didn't think he was going to answer her. Then he said, "Maybe I just liked the idea of having your blue blood running through the veins of my child."

"From what I've read in the tabloids, half the women you

keep company with have blood that's a lot bluer than mine,'' she told him coolly. "So why don't you tell me the real reason, Cole? Why would a man who's considered one of the country's most eligible bachelors want me to be the mother of his child?"

His mouth hardened. The skin across his cheekbones tightened. "Because you owe me, princess. You didn't want me or our baby."

Stung by his reply, Regan turned away from him; wrapped her arms around herself. "Want to hear something funny? For a minute I actually thought that maybe it was because you...that you might still..." She bit back the sob that rose in her throat.

How could she have been so foolish? Have allowed herself to think that Cole might still care for her? She'd been deluding herself. Just because she had never stopped loving Cole, didn't mean he still loved her.

"Regan, I—"

She flinched when he touched her shoulder. "I know you think I'm spoiled and selfish, Cole, but until now, I never realized that you thought I was so heartless." She drew in a shuddering breath. "I loved our baby," she said fiercely. "When I miscarried and lost our little girl, a part of me died, too. I wanted her. I wanted her so much. So very much." Tears streamed down her cheeks. It had been difficult enough losing Cole, but losing their baby meant she had lost her last link to him and the love they had shared.

"I'm sorry, princess."

She shrugged off the hand stroking her hair, finding no comfort in Cole's touch now. Feeling only the pain of realizing he thought her capable of destroying the child their love had created.

"I never really believed him. Deep inside, I knew he was lying. I was a fool to let him get to me, for even listening to his lies."

Swiping at her eyes, Regan turned around to face him. "What are you talking about? Listening to who—" She didn't bother finishing the question because from the disgust that etched sharp grooves beside his mouth, Regan knew. "My father," she said, her knees buckling at the shock.

Swearing, Cole caught her and carried her over to the couch, where he sat down and held her stiff body against him. When the trembling finally stopped, she freed herself from his arms and covered her face with her hands. Suddenly she felt a thousand years old and weary. "I can't believe that Daddy would tell you that I...that I didn't want the baby."

Anger reddened the sharp angles of Cole's cheeks while his eyes frosted, glittering like ice. "He said you regretted getting pregnant and having to marry me. You'd already told me you wanted an annulment, that you wanted your old life back. When he implied that the miscarriage wasn't an accident, I..."

"You believed him." Regan wasn't sure what hurt more—her father's ugly insinuations to ensure that Cole hated her or the fact that Cole thought her capable of such a thing. "Just for the record, it was a miscarriage."

"I'm sorry. More sorry than you can know. You have a right to be angry with me and I don't blame you. But it's in the past, princess," he said, catching her fingers and refusing to let go despite her protests. "We need to forget it and concentrate on the future. Our baby's future and our own."

"You and I don't have a future," she told him.

As though he hadn't heard her, Cole continued, "I've already talked to a judge who is a friend of mine, and he's agreed to waive the three-day waiting period for a wedding license."

Icy fury crystalized in Regan's veins, and she jerked her hands free. "I'm not marrying you."

His expression hardened. "What about Exclusives? Are you prepared to lose it?"

Regan's heart lurched in her chest at the idea of losing the store. But the thought of entering a loveless marriage with Cole would be far worse. She hiked her chin up, met his calculating gaze. "According to you, I've already lost it, since you own the mortgage."

A frown tugged at his mouth. "I'm willing to make a deal. You agree to marry me and live with me until the baby is born, then I'll sign over Exclusives to you free and clear."

"And what happens after the baby is born?"

"I'll agree to a quiet divorce and joint custody."

"That's all?" she asked warily.

"Just a few other minor conditions."

"Like what?" she countered.

"Like the fact that I'll expect you to be faithful to me throughout our marriage."

"What about you?" she asked, then could have bit off her tongue. His eyes darkened. He skimmed his gaze over her, then settled on her mouth. To her utter annoyance, Regan felt a flush of heat go through her body.

"Naturally, I'll be faithful to you, too."

"What else?" Regan asked.

"I want everyone to believe that our marriage and your pregnancy are the result of a love match. It's a matter of record that we were married when we were kids, so most people will believe it. I expect you to act the part of a loving bride."

Regan sucked in a sharp breath at the idea of pretending she and Cole were in love. He was offering her a chance to keep the promise she'd made to her father and to herself—to see that Exclusives continued and someday to pass it on to her own child. But suddenly the price of keeping those promises seemed far too high. "I don't think it's necessary for us to go that far. After all, Aunt Liz already knows the truth."

"All Liz knows is how our baby was conceived. You know as well as I do the reason she engineered me into being your sperm donor was because she thinks we still love each other."

"We don't." At least, Cole didn't love her, she amended.

"But no one except you and I know that. Just pretend you're playing a role in a play and remember that the payoff for a good performance will be Exclusives free of debt and yours to do with as you will."

It hurt to realize he believed her to be so shallow. But then, she had fostered that notion herself years ago when she had agreed to her father's demands, hadn't she? "Why the charade? What difference does it make if people believe we're in love with each other or not?"

"Because years from now I don't want our child to have any doubts that he or she was created out of love."

His response surprised her, humbled her. And also made her wonder if the rumors she'd heard years ago were true—that Cole was the result of some college boy's bet with his buddies that he could seduce the virginal Mary Beth Thornton. The sweet-tempered lady Regan remembered had succumbed to someone's charms, because she'd obviously given birth to Cole. But during the years that Regan knew her, Mary Beth Thornton had never had a husband. She'd always claimed she was still waiting for Mr. Right to come along. Regan thought back to the birth certificate Cole had produced when they'd crossed the state line into Mississippi to get married. All too clearly she recalled the space for his father's name on the document and the word *unknown* typed in the block. She'd known Cole had been ashamed of that fact. But she hadn't suspected until now just how great his shame had been, or how deeply the hurt ran knowing the circumstances behind his conception.

"So, what's it going to be, princess? Do we have a deal?"

"Yes. We have a deal."

* * *

He had the deal he wanted, Cole reminded himself, as he sat across the table from Regan in the five-star restaurant where he'd insisted she join him for dinner. With increasing annoyance he watched as she pored over the documents prepared by his attorney outlining the terms of their alliance. Regan had agreed to his marriage bargain. Now it was simply a matter of her signing the papers and the two of them setting a wedding date. He had won. She would be his wife when their child was born. So, why didn't he *feel* like he'd won?

Because he still wanted Regan. And wanting her made him weak.

He huffed out a breath at the admission. He'd known for weeks that the sexual chemistry was still there between them, maybe even stronger now than it had been twelve years ago. Judging by Regan's response to that last kiss they'd shared, the feeling was evidently mutual. But he didn't *want* to want her. He knew better than to follow through on the sexual attraction tugging at him. He'd already ruled out that option. Sleeping with Regan would only complicate things that were already far too complicated. He was marrying her for their baby's sake. Nothing more. Besides, he'd learned his lesson the last time he'd gotten involved with Regan, and he'd sworn then that he'd never let another woman tangle him up in knots the way she had.

So, dammit, why was he sitting here all hot and bothered, trying to talk himself out of taking her to bed and making their marriage in name only a real one?

Because somehow the lady managed to break into all those neat, safe compartments you've designated in your relationships for things like attraction, sex, friendship, affection. And now that she's broken into them, what are you going to do about it?

Not a thing, Cole vowed.

Right pal, the voice inside his head mocked. He didn't have a prayer of keeping that promise, not when just looking

at her had him hot, hard and hungry for her. Disgusted by
his own weakness, he swirled the brandy in his glass and
brooded over his predicament. He'd been with any number
of women far more beautiful than Regan. So why was it that
only she stirred desire in him so strong that it bordered on
desperation?

Because there's never been anyone else like her.

It was true, he admitted. She was unique—like the ala-
baster sculpture he kept in his bedroom. He had paid a king's
ransom for the piece—a miniature nude of a woman's lush
body stretching in sensual abandon, her delicate features
captured to perfection by the artist and frozen in a three-
dimensional glass frame.

Only, Regan St. Claire was no erotic fantasy carved in
cold stone and locked in a glass case to be admired and
never touched. Regan was real, a flesh-and-blood woman
full of passion and fire—passion and fire that he had tasted
once and had never forgotten. Tightening his fingers around
the brandy snifter, Cole recalled how warm and soft that
ivory skin of hers was, the way she quivered beneath his
hands. He took a sip of brandy and continued to study her
over the rim of his glass. He knew the simple black dress
she wore hadn't been chosen to instill lust in him. But that
didn't stop his fingers from itching to peel away the fabric
that molded her breasts and cup them in his palms. Dragging
his gaze upward, he stared at the long, slim neck, imagined
how the pulse there would flutter if he were to press his
mouth against it.

Heat jerked low in his belly, and he felt the tightening in
his groin. Shifting his attention to safer territory, he noted
the shafts of white gold that shimmered in the hair she'd
pulled into a coil at the back of her neck. For the space of
a heartbeat he was tempted to reach across the table, yank
out the confining pins and wrap his fists in all that blonde
silk. Tearing his thoughts from that tantalizing image, he
focused on that serious mouth of hers instead. Big mistake,

he realized too late as the savage need to taste those soft pink lips slammed through him with the force of a hurricane wind. Cole sucked in a breath. The truth was he wanted to do a hell of a lot more than just taste Regan's mouth, which only added to the frustration that had been gnawing in his gut for nearly a month now.

He wanted Regan, period, he admitted—in every way that a man can want a woman. And dammit, he wanted her to want him. Desperate to cool the fire burning in his blood, he tossed back the rest of the brandy, felt the liquid heat hit the back of his throat and blaze a trail down to his gut. Damn, he thought, slapping the glass down on the table when what he really wanted to do was smash the thing against a wall.

"Is there a problem?" Regan asked, lifting cool green eyes to meet his.

"Yeah, there's a problem." He was iron-hard and aching, and she was as cool and unaffected as fresh-fallen snow.

"And that problem is?"

"The problem is that you're going over that blasted thing like it's some kind of multi-national merger," he snarled, jutting his chin toward the agreement she held. "It's a simple contract. Not the Constitution."

"I realize that," she said calmly. "I just wanted to make sure that all the items we discussed are covered."

"What's the matter? Afraid I'll try to cheat you out of your precious store after all?"

"No. I simply don't want any surprises," she informed him.

That polite tone of hers tore another strip off his already fast-vanishing control, and he felt the perverse need to see her rattled the way he was. "Is that so? I seem to remember a time when you liked my surprises," he said, his voice deliberately soft, suggestive. Leaning closer, he dropped his voice to a whisper and reminded her of just how quickly he'd turned her shock into cries of pleasure when he had spread her thighs and made love to her with his mouth for the very first time.

Her pretty mouth opened, closed, and he had the satisfaction of seeing color flame in her cheeks. There was nothing calm and polite about the way she looked at him now. Eyes snapping with fury, she shoved back her chair and stood. "I'd like to go home—now."

Not bothering to wait for him, she started toward the exit. Quickly Cole dropped some bills on the table to cover the tab and a generous tip and then followed Regan.

Taunting her with that particular memory had been a dumb thing to do, Cole realized as he slid behind the wheel of his car a few minutes later, because remembering making love to Regan had whipped his own desire to a frenzied pitch and brought him right back to square one. What was he going to do about the fact that he wanted Regan in his bed?

In his bed? He nearly laughed out loud at how tame that sounded. It didn't even begin to describe how he felt. Hell, he wanted Regan anywhere. Everywhere. All the time. And as often as physically possible.

Tightening his grip on the steering wheel, Cole bit back a curse for torturing himself this way and tried to rein in his hormones. Judging by the militant tilt of Regan's chin, he wasn't going to be indulging in any of his sexual fantasies any time soon. But damn if he wasn't tempted to lean across the console and kiss that pout off her lips. As though sensing his scrutiny, she speared him with a quelling glance.

A horn blared from behind, and muttering a thing or two about impatient drivers, Cole directed his attention back to the road. But throughout the rest of the drive, he was conscious of the woman seated beside him and of the speculative looks she kept shooting his way—looks that didn't do a thing to ease the heavy ache in his loins.

By the time his sleek, black Mercedes headed down the driveway toward Regan's home, Cole admitted that any noble intentions he'd had about their marriage remaining one in name only weren't going to happen. Pulling the car to a stop, he shifted into Park and cut the engine.

"There's really no need for you to walk me to the door," she said, unhooking her seatbelt.

Ignoring the remark, Cole unfolded himself from his seat and walked around to open the door for her. When she hesitated to take the hand he offered, Cole smiled and said, "What's the matter, princess. Afraid I'll bite?"

"Hardly," she said with cool disdain as she placed her hand in his.

"Maybe you should be," he replied softly, dangerously.

"You can knock off the intimidation techniques. They're really a waste of time—and unnecessary," she said, her eyes shooting angry green sparks. Not giving an inch, she looked him square in the eye. "I've already agreed to go along with this phony marriage plan of yours."

Using his hold on her fingers, he drew her closer until her breasts brushed against the front of his jacket. At the swift stab of desire, everything in Cole demanded he haul her into his arms, claim that sassy mouth scowling at him and satisfy the hunger that had his gut twisted into a knot. He wanted to make love to her until their naked bodies were tangled together, sweating and sated. Viciously, he fought back the urge and said, "There won't be anything phony about this marriage, princess. It will be a real one—in every way."

Five

"**I** know the marriage will be real, at least legally," Regan explained, as she tugged her fingers free of Cole's. She took a step back, hating the retreat that action signaled, but needing physical distance so she could get her emotions in check. "What I meant was that the marriage is only going to be temporary and in name only."

"If by 'in name only' you're referring to no sex, I don't recall making that particular promise."

"But I…" Regan snapped her mouth closed, annoyed by the fact that Cole's threat of sex between them had her pulse stammering. She took a deep calming breath, reminded herself that she couldn't afford to fall under Cole's spell again. He was insisting on this marriage for the baby's sake—nothing more. Willing her pulse to slow, she tilt her chin up and said, "I think we'd better get something straight right now. I have no intention of sleeping with you."

"Actually, princess, sleep wasn't what I had in mind." His mouth kicked up at the corners into that grin that he'd used so sparingly, but effectively, to turn her teenaged knees to mush. "As I recall, the last time we were married, we did very little sleeping."

Regan felt the flush climb her neck at the none-too-subtle reminder that they had spent most of their short marriage in bed making love. "This isn't like the last time," she told him. And it wasn't. This time there was no love or even any pretense of love on Cole's part. He was marrying her simply to insure that their baby was born under the respectable banner of the Thornton name. She'd already resigned herself to that fact and was willing to go along with the sham wedding for Cole's sake. But that didn't stop the sharp pang of sadness from knifing through her. "Things are different now."

"Are they?" he asked in a low, sexy drawl that hinted at the years he'd lived in the South.

"You know they are." This time there were no words of love, no plans for a future together.

"Apparently not everything. I still want you, princess, and judging by the way you kissed me, you feel the same way."

Blast the man, Regan thought, irritated no end that he could still affect her so strongly. While she would like to blame the desire he ignited in her on hormonal changes caused by her pregnancy, she knew in her heart that wasn't true. She wanted Cole now, just as she had wanted him years ago and for the same reason. She loved him. But she'd be darned if she'd settle for sex as a substitute for his love. Hardening her resolve, she said coolly, "I don't recall my engaging in sex with you as one of the conditions in this marriage agreement."

"It isn't. But there's nothing in our agreement that says we can't have sex with each other if we want to. Personally," he said, toying with a strand of hair that had worked itself loose from her chignon, "I kind of like the idea of having you in my bed at night. And from those sideways glances you were giving me at the restaurant and in the car tonight, I suspect you like the idea, too."

"In your dreams, Thornton," she told him, slapping his hand away.

"Funny you should mention dreams," he murmured with a sensual glint in his eyes. "Because I've been having quite a few of them lately involving you. Want me to tell you about them?"

"No," she countered frostily. Shoving past him, she marched up the stairs of the veranda to the front door, eager to get away from Cole and from all the feelings he stirred up inside her. Feelings like love and desire and need.

By the time she'd managed to dig her key out of her purse and unlock the door, Regan had regained some measure of her composure. It was bad enough that he knew she was still attracted to him. How much worse would it be if he knew that she still loved him? It would be horrible because he would surely use it against her. Sensing his presence behind her, Regan braced herself before she turned to face him. The porch light accentuated the midnight black of his hair, the sharp angles of his face, the gleam of desire in the gray eyes. An answering heat curled low in her belly. Seeking a means to diffuse Cole's sensual impact to her senses, Regan said, "Thank you for dinner. The restaurant and the meal were lovely. And the evening was…interesting."

Cole laughed. "But the evening's not over yet."

"Actually it is—at least for me," she returned politely. No way did she intend to risk having him come inside—not when just looking at him had desire spinning in her veins. "I've had a long day, and I'm very tired. So I'll just say good-night."

But before she could turn away and escape inside, Cole's hand shot out. He flattened his palms against the doorframe, caging her between the door and his body. "Not so fast, princess."

Regan's pulse leaped. Her view narrowed until her field of vision was filled only with him, to the fit of the navy jacket that spanned his broad shoulders, to the crisp white shirt and patterned tie that hung loose around his open collar, to the deeply tanned column of his throat. All her senses tuned to him, she registered the warmth of his body mere centimeters from her own, the unique scent that belonged only to Cole.

He eased a fraction closer until his mouth was so close that his breath mingled with hers. "Aren't you forgetting something?"

Her heartbeat quickening, Regan fastened her eyes on Cole's mouth. His hot, tempting mouth. Liquid heat spilled through her as she waited for his kiss. A kiss that, she admitted, she wanted desperately. Barely breathing, her body humming in anticipation of that first brush of his mouth against hers, she could almost taste the brandy that lingered on his lips, on his tongue. She closed her eyes, tipped up her face to his.

But he didn't kiss her. Confused, she opened her eyes. Heat flooded her cheeks once again—this time in humiliation. Nearly choking in fury with herself, she snapped, "Exactly what is it you think I forgot?"

"The contract."

Regan clenched the envelope in her fist when he held out his hand. "I'll get it back to you later."

A perverse sense of satisfaction shot through her when he narrowed his eyes. "Why not sign it now? You spent most of the evening studying the thing."

"I know. But I want my attorney to go over it before I sign it."

His expression sobered. "Why? Is there a problem?"

"No. At least none that I noticed." Other than the fact that she was about to marry the man she loved, the man who was the father of the baby she carried, and that man not only didn't love her but he didn't trust her to keep her word. "As a businessman, I'm sure you'd agree that it would be foolish of me to sign any legal documents without having my attorney review them."

"This isn't a business deal," he countered with a scowl.

"Funny, that's what it looks and sounds like to me."

"You know what I mean."

"Yes, I do, and that's why I'm not signing anything until I go over it with my attorney first."

"Fine," he told her with none of the teasing warmth or charm he'd bombarded her with all evening. "Just make sure I have it back with your signature tomorrow by noon."

"By noon?" she said, astonished. "But that's not enough time. I'm not even sure I can get an appointment with my attorney that quickly."

"Then that's your problem, princess. Because it's all the time you've got."

"Fine," she spat out the word. "You'll have it back by noon."

"With your signature."

"With my signature…barring my attorney finds any complications," she amended.

"He won't."

"Now if you'll excuse me, I'll say good-night."

She waited for him to move so that she could go inside. When he didn't, she shot a glance up to his face. He smiled at her, his teeth a flash of white against his deeply tanned skin. "Aren't you going to kiss me good-night?"

"I don't think that would be a good idea."

"Sure it would," he told her, running his knuckles along her jaw. "After all, very soon, you'll be my wife again."

"Your wife in name only," she reminded him.

"Yes, well," he eased even closer. "Why don't I see if I can change your mind about that?"

Regan retreated a step until her back pressed against the door. Sliding her free hand behind her, she clutched at the doorknob, twisted it. Relief washed through her when she felt it give under her hand. Pride had her angle up her chin and meet his gaze. "Oh, I'd really hate to see you bother— since I have no intention of changing my mind." Giving the door a little shove, she stepped back into the safety of her home and closed the door in his face.

After turning the lock, Regan leaned against the door. Her heart racing with a combination of excitement and nerves, she stared at the crumpled envelope she still held in her fist. The phone shrilled, echoing in the silence of the big house. Regan ignored it and struggled to rein in her emotions. She couldn't lose sight of the reason Cole wanted to marry her— not if she hoped to survive the next six months with her heart intact. Because there was no question in her mind that Cole would break her heart all over again—if she let him. For her sake and their baby's, she couldn't give him that chance.

The phone stopped ringing, and the empty silence that descended over the house emphasized more acutely just how alone she felt. Suddenly fatigued both physically and emotionally, Regan turned off the outdoor lights and headed for her bedroom. As she mounted the sweeping staircase, she was struck not for the first time by the overwhelming size of her home. While the St. Claire mansion was beautiful, and she appreciated the history of her ancestors who had lived here before her, the place had been her father's showcase, not hers. She thought again how she would have much preferred a normal house growing up—a place where she could run and play, where she could plop down on a chair without fearing it was a priceless antique that might break.

As she reached the landing, the phone started ringing again. Probably her Aunt Liz or Maggie checking up on her, she thought, only now realizing that she had promised to call them both tonight after her dinner with Cole. She hurried into her bedroom, tossed her purse and the envelope on the bed, then reached for the receiver. "Hello."

"You all right, princess?"

Her pulse kicked at the sound of Cole's voice. The fatigue that had triggered her melancholy evaporated immediately and adrenaline surged through her system again.

"Regan?"

"I'm fine," she replied. Kicking off her heels, she reached for the switch on the lamp beside her bed.

"Just wanted to make sure. I didn't see the light go on in your bedroom."

Her fingers froze over the switch momentarily before flicking it on. Soft light flooded the room and chased away the shadows. "Where are you?"

"Downstairs, watching your bedroom window."

Unable to resist, Regan moved to the windows and pulled back the drape. He stood in the distance, a tall dark figure leaning against his black car, his gaze trained on her bedroom while he spoke into the cell phone. "Why?"

"Since I haven't seen any servants, I assume you don't have a live-in staff anymore, and that you're alone in that old mausoleum."

"Is there a point in there somewhere?"

"The point is you shouldn't be alone in your condition."

Regan expelled a breath. "I'm pregnant, Cole. Not ill."

"But suppose something happened? You could fall, get sick again…what if something happened to the baby?"

Regan released the curtain, turned away from the window and squeezed her eyes shut a moment. She knew she had no right to feel the stab of disappointment that Cole's concern had been for the baby and not her. But darn it, her heart just didn't seem to care. Because she wanted Cole to care about her, too. "Everything's fine, Cole. You can go."

After a long pause, he said, "All right. But promise you'll call if you need me."

"I promise. Good-night."

"Princess?"

"Yes?"

"Don't forget, I want you with the signed contract at my hotel tomorrow by noon."

"I won't forget."

* * *

But either Regan did forget or she had no intention of showing up at all, Cole concluded, when she had yet to make an appearance by twelve-thirty. "You still haven't heard from her?" Cole asked, annoyed by the timid creature on the other end of the phone line at Exclusives.

"No, Mr. Thornton, I haven't. As I explained earlier, Ms. St. Claire said she had some business to take care of and that she wouldn't be in today. So I don't expect to hear from her."

"If you *do* hear from her, tell her to call me," Cole said before slamming down the telephone receiver.

"Take it easy, Cole. She's only a little late," his attorney and friend Jack Stewart reminded him.

Cole scowled across the table at the golden-haired ivy-leaguer who had been his friend for more than ten years—a fact that still amazed him sometimes since Jack's privileged background was the antithesis of Cole's own. "She's not supposed to be late," Cole informed him in a voice that would have made most men shudder in their boots.

Jack's Gucci loafers didn't even twitch. "Evidently she doesn't know that."

"I made it clear to her that she had to be here by noon."

"Or what? You'll call off the wedding?" Jack asked while he calmly poured himself another cup of the city's dark, rich coffee-and-chicory brew. He took a sip, sighed with pleasure. "From what little you've told me about the lady, I got the distinct impression that she isn't all that keen on becoming your wife as it is."

Which was the reason he was so uptight, Cole conceded. Regan didn't want to marry him. She'd made that fact perfectly clear, and he knew that the only reason she had finally agreed to do so was because he'd backed her into a corner by holding the mortgage on Exclusives as hostage. No way was she willing to walk away from her birthright. Or at least she hadn't been willing to walk away from it. After last night, he was no longer so sure.

He'd crossed the line, Cole admitted. And he might have blown everything. He knew without her saying a word that he had gone way beyond the boundaries of fair play when he'd pressed her to go to bed with him. But dammit, he hadn't expected to be so susceptible to her again. No way had he thought he would be in any danger of falling under her spell a second time, or of finding himself ensnared by a pair of innocent-looking green eyes and sweet-smelling skin. He hadn't anticipated being haunted by dreams of Regan naked beneath him or of finding himself in a constant state of arousal whenever she was around. He certainly hadn't realized that the woman would muddle his brain until he'd almost forgotten that the baby was the reason he wanted this marriage in the first place. A *temporary* marriage, he corrected, assuming there would even be a marriage at all.

"How is it you've never mentioned this Regan to me before?"

"Since when do I need to clear my social life with you?" Cole fired back.

Jack arched his brow in surprise. "My, my. We are a bit testy, aren't we?"

"No, we are not testy," Cole practically snarled. "We are annoyed."

Jack sat back in the chair, an amused look in his brown eyes. "I don't think I've ever seen you quite so rattled before, Thornton. And certainly never by a female."

"I'm not rattled," Cole countered. "I told you I'm annoyed because she's late."

"Uh-huh. And I'm growing more intrigued by the mysterious Ms. St. Claire by the minute. In fact, I think I may be well on my way to falling in love with the lady."

Cole snorted, but a knot of jealousy fisted in his gut. "For all you know she looks like a mule."

"Oh, I doubt that. Despite your faults, you have exceptional taste when it comes to women."

"I'm so happy you approve."

Jack grinned, his even teeth a flash of white in his cover boy face. "Oh, I approve. And after all the years of watching females throw themselves at your feet, I'm actually enjoying watching you sweat over a woman who isn't taken in by that ugly mug of yours. It does this poor country lawyer's heart—"

"Poor country lawyer?" Cole sputtered at the outrageous lie. "Since when is John Paul Stewart, V, of the prestigious Boston Stewarts and a member of the firm of Stewart & Sons considered poor?"

Jack shrugged. "Hey, the fact that my family's money is a few hundred years older than yours doesn't change the fact that you've got a lot more of it than I do."

Cole almost grinned. "I guess there is that," he told Jack, the man he considered his best friend since he had accepted him and all the skeletons in his closet long before Cole had made his first fortune.

"And in case you've forgotten, *I'm* the one who's the working stiff here. Not you. Which means I intend to bill you for every minute of my *very* expensive time. Plus expenses. And don't expect any discounts. You're being charged the firm's full rate for insisting I drop everything and hotfoot it here to New Orleans."

This time Cole did grin, his foul mood lightening a bit. "Hopefully I'll be able to scrape up the cash to pay you."

Jack laughed. "That shouldn't be too much of a problem. Selling off a few of your smaller companies should take care of my bill. The truth is, pal, it's almost worth forgoing my outrageous fee just to see the mighty Cole Thornton, the man who's made dodging marriage an art form, take the fall. And that's some hefty wedding gift you're giving the bride— paying off the mortgage on her store. If I didn't know better, I might think you'd resorted to blackmail to get the lady to marry you."

Cole beat back the flicker to his conscience, remembering Regan had accused him of the very same thing. "The lady could have said no," he informed Jack. "And for all I know she *has* said no since she still isn't here."

"So what are you going to do if she has changed her mind?"

Suddenly all the worries and doubts came tumbling back. "How the hell do I know? I certainly don't plan to hold a gun to the woman's head to force her to marry me."

"I can't tell you how glad I am to hear that."

Cole spun around, spied Regan standing in the doorway, looking cool, calm, regal—just the opposite of the way he was feeling. He moved his gaze over her, took in the pale pink dress she wore, noted the way it brought out the luster of her skin and the vivid green of her eyes. He scanned her face in an attempt to register her mood. He couldn't, but he didn't miss the hint of shadows beneath her eyes or that her lush mouth was unsmiling.

"You must be Regan," Jack said, all smiles as he walked over to her. Cole didn't miss the appreciative gleam in his friend's eye as he reached for her hand and kissed her fingers. "I can't tell you how very pleased I am to finally meet you. I'm Jack Stewart, by the way, a friend of the bridegroom as well as his attorney."

"How do you do, Mr. Stewart?"

"Jack," he corrected smoothly. "My friends call me Jack, and, my dear Regan, I do hope you and I are going to be friends."

"Knock it off, Stewart, or you'll find yourself with one less friend and client," Cole muttered, irritated by the sight of his suave friend charming Regan.

Jack arched his brow at the threat, but released Regan's hand. "You'll have to forgive Cole. The man's a bit of a grouch today, and I suspect it's your fault."

"My fault?"

"He was afraid you weren't going to show."

"That's enough, Stewart," Cole said in a voice designed

to tear a strip off his cocky friend. He slapped his eyes back to Regan. "You were supposed to be here by noon."

The warmth in her eyes faded. She hiked up her chin. "You'll have to excuse me for being late. But my attorney was tied up in court most of the morning," she said, her voice frosting over. "She wasn't able to meet me until almost eleven."

"Is the contract signed?"

"No."

The knot of tension that had formed in his stomach that morning as he'd waited for Regan to arrive wound even tighter. Now that she'd called his bluff, what was he going to do? He had no intention of shutting down her store. Never had. But—

"Did your attorney find a problem with the document?" Jack asked, a frown knitting his brow.

"Oh, no. Not at all. In fact, she said it was not only fair, but that the offer of child support and a trust fund for the baby was extremely generous." She shifted her gaze to Cole. "I guess I didn't read the contract as closely as I should have last night so I didn't realize you planned to establish a trust fund. Thank you, Cole. That was very thoughtful."

Cole nodded, more pleased than he wanted to be by her praise. "So if there's nothing wrong with the contract, why haven't you signed it?"

"I wasn't sure, but I thought maybe I should sign it in front of witnesses."

Cole told himself it wasn't relief that had the knots of tension in his neck easing or his chest feeling like a weight had been lifted from it. He didn't want to believe that Regan's willingness to marry him could trigger such a reaction in him. Yet he couldn't recall the last time that he had felt like hauling a woman into his arms to kiss her and spin her around in circles.

Not that he had any intention of doing those things with

Regan. It was one thing to desire her. But it was quite another to trust her. He'd made the mistake of trusting her once. It wasn't a mistake he intended to repeat. He was marrying Regan for their baby's sake—nothing more, he told himself again.

"The lady's not only beautiful, Thornton, but she's smart."

Regan's cheeks pinked at the compliment. "Thank you. That's very kind of you, Mr. Stewart."

"Jack," he corrected.

"Jack," she repeated.

"And kindness has nothing to do with it. Cole's a very lucky man."

But he didn't feel the least bit lucky, Cole admitted, as Regan smiled at Jack with an easiness that had jealousy clawing at him. "If you two are finished with the mutual admiration society, maybe we can get down to business."

Jack gave an exaggerated sigh. "I do hope you realize what an impatient man you're marrying."

"Don't worry, Regan knows all my sins. Don't you, princess?"

"And you still want to marry this guy?" Jack joked.

Cole tensed. The breath froze in his lungs as he waited for her response. "Yes, I want to marry him."

"And here I thought you were a smart lady. You sure I can't convince you to dump this lug and marry me instead?" Jack teased.

"I said to knock it off," Cole warned, a sharp edge in his voice.

Regan laughed. "Thank you, Jack. I'm flattered. But I'm afraid the answer's no."

Jack placed a hand against his heart in mock disappointment. "Guess I'll just have to soothe my broken heart with all the ladies who are going to be mourning the loss of Thornton here on the bachelor market."

"If you don't cut the bull and get down to business, the

only one anybody's going to be mourning is you—at your funeral.'' With a proprietary hand at Regan's back, Cole led her over to the table and pulled out a chair.

Within moments Jack had produced a folder with several copies of the marriage contract, and after going over each point and asking if they had any questions, he indicated where they should sign and handed them each a pen.

Not until Regan had signed all of the copies and handed them back to Jack to be notarized was Cole finally able to breathe easily again.

''Well, that should do it,'' Jack said as he packed the signed contracts away in his briefcase and snapped the black leather attaché closed. ''Congratulations, again.''

Cole shook his hand. ''Thanks.''

''It was a pleasure meeting you, Regan. I can understand now why Cole is so eager to marry you.''

''Thank you,'' Regan murmured.

''And all kidding aside, Cole's one of the finest men I know. You couldn't have picked a better man to be your husband.''

''I know,'' she said, her voice softening.

A rush of pleasure shot through Cole at her response. He stared at Regan. For a moment, he could almost believe she'd meant it.

''…and don't forget, I expect an invitation to the wedding and at least one dance with the bride.''

Cole jerked his attention back to the conversation. ''You'll get an invitation,'' he assured his friend as he ushered him out of the suite, but he made no such promise about that dance with Regan. Once he closed the door behind Jack, Cole turned around to face Regan.

''I'd better be going, too,'' she told him, gathering her handbag. ''I haven't been into the store yet today.''

''I was under the impression you were taking the day off.''

''Yes. Well, I wasn't sure how long this would take. But

now that everything's finished, I think I'll go in. I have several orders that need completing, plus some paperwork that needs my attention.''

Walking over to her, Cole removed the purse she held in a death grip from her fingers and placed it on the table. He took her stiff hands in his. ''The work can wait a bit longer, can't it?''

She pulled her hands free. ''Actually, it can't. I really am behind, and I—''

''We need to talk, princess. We have some decisions to make.''

''But we covered everything in the contract,'' she argued.

''Not quite everything.''

At the rush of color in her cheeks, Cole suspected she was remembering their conversation last night. What would have happened if he had kissed her as he'd wanted to do last night? And how would she respond now if he led her into the bedroom and sealed their marriage agreement the way he wanted to—by removing that pretty pink dress she was wearing and making love to her?

The urgency to do just that was so powerful it shook him. He'd be better off not finding out, he decided, because he didn't want to risk having her back out of their agreement. And, he admitted, because he wasn't sure if he made love to Regan that he would be able to keep his promise and let her go when the time came to end their marriage. No, he assured himself. He was better off suffering a bit of sexual frustration now than putting himself through the hell of having her walk away from him a second time. And she would walk. He knew that as sure as he knew his name.

''What is it that still needs discussing?''

Cole nearly smiled at the challenging tilt of her chin. ''For starters—the wedding. We need to settle on a date, decide how big or small an affair we want, where we're going to hold the ceremony and reception.''

Losing some of the starch in her spine, Regan eyed him warily. "I haven't given it a lot of thought. I just assumed you wouldn't want a big fuss. I mean, we both know you're marrying me because of the baby."

"Just as we both know that you're marrying me because you want Exclusives." Not bothering to wait for her to refute the claim, he asked, "Have you eaten lunch yet?"

"No. But—"

"Neither have I. I'll order something from room service," he said, picking up the phone. "We can work out the details while we eat."

"Cole, I'm really not hungry."

"Hungry or not, you still need to eat, princess."

"But—"

"For the baby's sake," he insisted and proceeded to order them both a full meal.

Nearly an hour later, after Regan had managed to put away her own lunch and the better part of his, Cole sat back and stared at the woman with amusement. "For a lady who wasn't hungry, you did a credible job of impersonating someone who was starving," he teased.

"I did, didn't I?" she responded sheepishly, a grin curving her lips. "I keep telling myself it's the pregnancy that's making me eat like this. And I hope that's true because I seem to be hungry all the time lately. Would you mind terribly ordering some more milk? I've never been much of a milk drinker, but lately I just can't seem to get enough of the stuff."

"Not a problem," he assured her and ordered a pitcher of fresh coffee and more milk to be sent up to the suite. When he hung up the phone and turned his attention back to Regan, she was finishing the last of the strawberries that had garnished her salad plate. Cole shook his head. "What

I want to know is where do you put it all? You don't even look pregnant.''

"Maybe I don't look pregnant to you, but I certainly can see the difference. And if I keep eating like this, I'm going to be the size of a moose before I reach my sixth month.''

"Impossible. You could never resemble a moose.''

Something in his tone must have made her nervous because she pushed to her feet. "Maybe we should move over to the couch while we wait for the milk. Otherwise, I'm liable to start gnawing on the china.''

"You have a point,'' he told her as he followed her over to the sectional sofa.

"I know,'' she said as she sank down to the velvety cushions with a laugh that lit up her face and made her eyes sparkle. "I can barely button my skirts now as it is.''

"You look just fine to me,'' he said, sliding his gaze over her body.

"You won't think so when I start to waddle because my stomach's out to here.''

Suddenly the image of Regan's belly all round and swollen with his child made Cole's heart pound in his chest. "I think that's when you'll be most beautiful.''

Regan's smile faded. Her fingers curled into the skirt of her dress. "You know, I didn't realize how late it was, and I really do need to get into the shop. Maybe we better get those details about the wedding out of the way now.''

"All right,'' Cole conceded, stamping down on the burst of desire and tenderness. "Why don't we start off with what type of wedding you want?''

"I just assumed we would do something simple.''

"You settled for simple and cheap the last time when we eloped. You were cheated of the big splash your father would have given you if you'd married someone besides me. You don't have to skimp this time. You can have whatever type of wedding you want and I'll pay for it.''

"That's not necessary, Cole. We can share the expense."

He pressed a finger against her lips. "I'm paying for the wedding, princess. No arguments. And I can afford to give you as big and as splashy a wedding as you want."

"But I don't *want* a big wedding. I never did. I'd rather something small and intimate with just Aunt Liz and a few close friends."

"You're sure?"

"Positive."

"All right. Small and intimate it is." But Cole couldn't help wondering if Regan would have chosen differently if she were marrying him because she loved him and not simply to save her business. It didn't matter, he told himself, and tried to shake off the brooding thoughts.

"What about you?" she asked, a frown line forming across her brow.

"A small wedding is fine with me."

"I'm glad," she said on a sigh. "I'm not sure I could handle a crush of people."

"You won't have to. Now how do you feel about having the ceremony in that little chapel you used to go to on Sundays when you were a kid?"

Surprise lit her eyes. "I'd like that."

"Then that's where we'll hold the ceremony." He reached for her left hand, uncurled her fingers. Then withdrawing the diamond ring from his pocket, he slipped it onto her finger. "I had hoped to give you this last night, but the evening didn't end as I'd hoped it would."

She stared at the flawless four-carat marquis set in a gold band. When she glanced up at him, tears swam in her eyes. "An engagement ring isn't necessary," she told him, her voice trembling.

"Do you like it?"

"How could I not like it? It's beautiful." She looked

down at the ring again. "I'll return it when…after the baby comes."

"The ring's yours," he told her, disturbed by the thought of ending their marriage before it had even begun. A surge of possessiveness filled him. He wanted to brand Regan as his—not just with his ring on her finger, but with his mouth, with his hands, with his sex buried deep inside her. He was a fool, Cole admitted. To want her like this. She'd been a fire in his blood once and would be again if he wasn't careful.

Promising himself he would be careful, Cole speared his fingers through hers and tugged Regan toward him. He heard her breath catch as her breasts came up against his chest. He watched as her green eyes turned smoky, her lips parted. Desire fisted in his gut. Groaning, Cole brought his mouth down on hers.

Biting back the urge to plunder, he kissed her slowly, tenderly, thoroughly. He swept his tongue over her mouth, exploring her, memorizing her. When he nipped her bottom lip with his teeth, she gasped and opened to him. He deepened the kiss. Regan's fingers fisted in his hair. She arched her back, pressing her body closer as she returned his kiss.

He was insane, Cole told himself as he streaked his hands down her back, palmed her bottom, then smoothed over her hips and lower along the curve of her knees. He navigated the hem of her dress, eased his fingers up the silky hose at the top of her thighs and moved higher until he cupped the heart of her heat. Shaking with the need to bury himself inside her, Cole tore his mouth free and forced himself to wait, telling himself he had to give her a choice. "Open your eyes and look at me," he ordered, his voice hoarse and gruff with need.

A breath shuddered through her. She swiped her tongue over her lips—lips that were ripe, swollen from his kisses, and Cole thought he might die with the effort it took not to kiss her again. Finally, her eyes fluttered open.

"I want you. But I need you to tell me that this is what you want, too."

"I—"

"Say it, princess. Tell me you want me."

"I—"

A fist rapped on the door. "Room service."

Six

Regan snatched her hands from Cole's shoulders where her fingers had been clutched in his shirt. "I…I can't do this," she told him, scrambling back to the corner of the couch and trying to straighten her clothes.

"Can't, or won't?" he countered, a sharp edge in his voice.

Regan met the cold steel gaze, knowing she deserved his contempt for reneging on what she'd been promising him with her lips only a moment ago. "It doesn't matter. Either way, the answer is still no."

Another rap of knuckles sounded at the door, followed by the barked, "room service." Swearing, Cole shoved off the couch and headed for the door.

The moment he was gone, Regan fled to the bathroom. Mortified by how close she'd come to making love with him. She leaned over the sink and splashed cold water on her face and wrists.

that had saved him from that hell. And even though things were different now, he didn't kid himself, marrying and letting her go a second time wouldn't be easy. A sane man wouldn't risk putting himself through that kind of turmoil. But each time he had wavered, thoughts of the baby had weighed in and he'd known he had to see this through.

"Uh, Cole, old buddy, you need to move it now. Father Weston says we should take our places."

"Tell him I'll be right there. I need a minute."

"Sure thing," Jack said and slipped back inside the chapel.

Cole turned back to Liz. "You heard the man, I need to get moving."

"And I need to check on Regan, see if she needs any help."

"So what was it you wanted to tell me?" he asked.

"I have a message for you from your mother."

His mother.

He'd forgotten all about his mother and her husband arriving this afternoon, Cole realized guiltily. He'd been so caught up in his worries about Regan and the wedding that he hadn't even bothered to check to see if she'd arrived at the hotel. While he'd arranged for a limo to meet her and her husband at the airport, transport them to the hotel and then to the chapel and reception, he still should have called her. "Did she and Al get in okay?"

A sad expression crossed Liz's face. "I'm sorry, dear. She and your stepfather won't be able to make the wedding after all. One of their boys won his school's swim meet and that made him eligible for a championship match tomorrow in another part of the state. They need to drive down this evening for the race."

"I see," Cole said, refusing to allow himself to feel disappointed. He'd been surprised when his mother had said she would come in the first place. She had a new life with a husband and two teenage sons, he reminded himself. He was happy for her and glad life was good for her now after all the years she'd had to struggle alone because of him. And after all, he was the visible reminder of his mother's youthful mistake and shame—a fact that no amount of success or money could ever change.

"She said she tried to reach you at your hotel and on your cell phone, but couldn't. So she called me and asked that I give you her apologies. She sends her love and best wishes."

"Guess I shouldn't have turned off my cell phone, huh?"

Liz touched his arm. "I'm sorry, Cole."

He shrugged. "It's no big deal. I understand." And he did. It was because he understood what it meant not to belong, not to fit in, that he knew insisting that Regan marry him had been the right thing to do for their child.

"I'm sure she would be here if she could," Liz offered in an obvious effort to console him.

"Of course she would."

"I'm sorry I had to be the bearer of bad news."

The distress in Liz's voice had his chest tightening again. Uncomfortable with how vulnerable it made him feel, he looped an arm around her shoulder. "Hey, come on now. No long faces on my wedding day. My mother bowing out is really no big deal," he assured her with a smile. "I'm fine. Or I will be as long as the bride doesn't change her mind and decide not to go through with the wedding."

She couldn't go through with the wedding.

Regan clutched her ivory wedding veil in her hands. Now that it was almost too late, she could see with startling clarity that marrying Cole was a mistake. She could hear the organist playing. The chapel was filled with guests expecting her to exit this private room at the back of the church, walk down the aisle and become Cole's wife. Only now she realized that she simply couldn't go through with it. She must have been insane to think she could marry Cole, live with him as husband and wife for six months, and then divorce

him after the baby was born. Her hands trembled. So did
her knees. She sank to the chair in front of the dressing table,
heedless of the resulting creases to the ivory crinoline skirt
of her dress. A bubble of hysteria rose in her throat. It didn't
matter if her dress became creased or not. She didn't have
to worry about a rumpled skirt in the wedding pictures because there weren't going to be any wedding pictures since
there wasn't going to be any wedding—at least not hers and
Cole's.

Oh God, how had she ever convinced herself that marrying Cole was the logical thing to do? The wedding was a
disaster in the making. Baby or no baby, she should never
have allowed Cole to bully her into agreeing to marry him.

A breath shuddered through her. In all fairness, she
couldn't place the blame for her predicament on anyone's
doorstep but her own. Logic and threats hadn't had a thing
to do with her agreeing to marry Cole. She'd done so for
the simple reason that she loved him. Only now, when it
was almost too late, did she realize what a terrible injustice
she'd be doing them both by going through with the wedding.

"Regan, darling," Liz said, breezing into the room, bringing the scent of jasmine and sunshine with her. "Why on
earth are you sitting there? You'll crease your pretty dress.
Never mind. What happened to your veil? Did the pins come
loose?"

"Aunt Liz, I can't do it."

"Don't worry, dear. I'll fix it for you. But we need to
hurry. The wedding's going to start any minute." She
plucked the veil from Regan's hand. "Now turn around and
let me see what I can do."

More out of habit than anything else, Regan obeyed and
turned to face the mirror. With the efficiency of a master
stylist, her aunt fitted the veil atop her head and began weav-
ing the pearl-studded pins that had belonged to her mother
into her hair.

"Wait until you see the chapel. It's breathtaking. So many magnolias and white roses and daisies. All your guests are here. And the groom, of course," she continued as she secured the veil with additional pins. "I just saw him a few minutes ago—looking much too handsome for his own good, I might add. And that friend Jack of his looked quite dashing, too. He seems quite smitten with Maggie. I understand the girl's turning her nose up at those stuffed-shirts her parents keep throwing in her path, but how she could be immune to such a charming young man as Jack…well, I don't understand. It's a pity I'm not thirty years younger."

Her aunt's happy chatter only underscored the sense of dread Regan was feeling at the prospect of announcing that she wasn't going to marry Cole after all. "Aunt Liz—"

"There now. All done." Her aunt stepped back, surveyed her handiwork and then said, "Oh, Regan, you make such a lovely bride. If only your parents were here to see you."

At the mention of her parents and the hint of tears in her aunt's voice, a lump the size of a baseball lodged in Regan's throat. She sucked in a deep breath. "Aunt Liz, you don't understand. I can't go through with the wedding. I can't marry Cole."

"Of course, you're going to marry him, darling. You've just got a few bridal jitters. That's all. And it's perfectly understandable considering how fast everything has happened between you."

"It's not bridal jitters, Aunt Liz. I'm serious. I thought I could marry Cole…for the baby's sake. Honestly, I did. But I can't go through with it. Not even for the baby."

Her aunt's serious brown eyes met her own in the mirror. "And is the baby really the reason you agreed to marry him?"

"You know the baby's the reason Cole insisted we get married."

"I know that's what you both claim. But you never answered my question, Regan. Is the baby the only reason you agreed to marry Cole?''

"No," Regan admitted. "I agreed to marry him because I love him. I've never stopped loving him. But that doesn't mean that marrying him is the right thing to do for either of us. It isn't. It's a mistake.''

Her aunt smoothed a hand over Regan's head. A wistful smile curved her lips. "Being in love with the man whose child you're carrying sounds like a pretty good reason to get married to me.''

"Not if he doesn't love me," Regan protested.

"Are you so sure that he doesn't?''

Regan thought of the contract that she'd signed and of her promise to Cole not to reveal even to her aunt that their marriage would only be a temporary one. So she couldn't explain that her aunt's romantic notions about Cole still loving her were wrong. He didn't love her. If he did, he wouldn't have already planned the end of their marriage before it had even begun. "Cole's marrying me out of a sense of duty—not love. It's a question of him honoring his responsibilities.''

"Which says a lot about the type of man he is. Not all men would accept the responsibility for a child conceived the way this one was.''

"I know." And she did. Cole was a good man. He'd accepted full responsibility when she'd gotten pregnant years ago, even though she had been equally at fault. He hadn't hesitated to marry her and had even taken on a second job in anticipation of having a wife and child to support. Of course, neither of them had counted on her father's determination to separate them, and neither of them had foreseen that she would lose the baby.

"Cole can be too serious sometimes, and I think he keeps far too much bottled up inside him. But that doesn't mean his feelings don't run deep. How do you think he's going to feel if you march out there and tell him that you're not going to marry him after all?''

He would feel the same way he had the last time she had walked away from him and claimed she didn't want to be his wife. He would feel angry. Betrayed. Hurt. Shamed. And he would hate her.

''And knowing the circumstances of his own birth and how seriously he takes his responsibilities, how do you think he's going to feel when you refuse to marry him and deny his child the very legitimacy that Cole has always wanted for himself? Can you truly love him and do that to him?''

She couldn't hurt him that way, Regan realized. But what about her? How did she protect her own heart?

The first strains of the wedding march began to play, and her aunt hustled her to the door. ''Whether you go through with the wedding or not is up to you. But few of us get a second chance, Regan. Make sure you don't toss away yours simply because you're afraid.''

Regan stared at the bridal bouquet that rested on the table by the door. Baby's breath, sprigs of ivy and satin ribbons were woven into the cascade of white roses and daisies. The same blossoms Cole had purchased for her the first time they had married. Daisies because they were her favorites, he'd claimed, and white roses because they were elegant and classy like her.

''Well, dear? What are you going to do?''

Regan picked up the bouquet, clutched it firmly in her hands. Squaring her shoulders, she said, ''I'm going to get married.''

Seven

Ignoring the guests who occupied a dozen or so pews, Cole fixed his gaze on the rear of the chapel. He barely noticed the white bows that were anchored at the end of each row or the rose petals that lay scattered along the length of the aisle runner. If pressed, Cole wasn't sure he could even identify a single flower used in the dozens of arrangements that filled every corner of the tiny church—flowers for which his secretary assured him he had paid a small fortune. Even the sound of the bridal march barely penetrated his brain, because every ounce of his attention remained focused on that doorway. The muscles in his neck and shoulders screamed from the tension that had held him in its grip all day. Yet he didn't move. He barely breathed while he waited, wondering if Regan would show up.

Not until she appeared at the center of the doorway did Cole actually allow himself to believe that she was going through with the wedding. For the first time in two weeks, he took a full breath—only to have the air back up in his lungs as Regan started down the aisle. She was a vision draped in ivory silk and clutching a fistful of white roses and daisies.

As she moved in slow, measured steps toward him, Cole took in every detail of her appearance—the luster of tiny pearls sewn into the top of the ivory dress she wore, the way the fabric skimmed her breasts and waist before falling in whisper-thin layers of something silky that swished around her ankles. She'd worn her hair up and tucked beneath a veil of matching ivory silk, but several blonde wisps had escaped and curled loosely about her face. Diamond and pearl earrings that reminded him of teardrops hung from her ears. She managed to look fragile yet brave and innocent all at the same time.

She had almost reached the end of the runner before Cole noticed that the bouquet she held was trembling slightly. His gaze zoomed up to her face. Her green eyes were wide and had that frightened look that reminded him of a deer caught in the headlights of a car. And except for the pale rose lipstick she wore, her face held little more color than her dress.

Cole didn't know why he suddenly descended the altar to meet her as he did—whether it was because he still didn't trust her not to bolt or because he simply couldn't bear to see the stress swimming in her eyes. But when he offered her his hand, she took it, clung to it like a lifeline. He returned the pressure on her fingers with a squeeze and led her up the stairs of the altar to stand before the minister.

"Dearly beloved," the minister began.

Cole tuned the man out almost immediately. He tuned out everything except for Regan and the fact that she was actually about to become his wife—again. He couldn't help but remember the last time they'd married. There had been no family, no friends, no music or candles. There had been no quaint chapel filled with flowers and ribbons. No minister to pray over them and ask God's blessing on their union. There had only been the cramped office of a justice of the peace and the paltry bouquet of white roses and daisies he'd picked up at a supermarket for her to carry.

She had deserved so much better than the quick, no-frills ceremony. He had sworn to her and to himself that someday he would make it up to her, that he would see that she had a proper wedding with all the trimmings. Only he had never dreamed that when he finally did make good on that promise, it would be with the knowledge that the vows they were about to take would only be temporary.

Lost in thoughts of the past, Cole didn't even realize that the minister had been speaking to him until Regan squeezed his fingers. He jerked his attention back to the minister who said, "Do you, Cole Thornton, take Regan St. Claire to be your wedded wife, to love and to cherish, in sickness and in health, for richer or poorer, until death do you part?"

"I do."

"And do you, Regan St. Claire, take Cole Thornton to be your wedded husband, to love and to cherish, in sickness and in health, for richer or poorer, until death do you part?"

"I do," she replied, her voice soft, but steady. And from the way she looked at him as she said the words, Cole could almost believe she meant them. For the first time since he'd learned she was carrying his baby and had decided they should marry for the child's sake, Cole allowed himself to wonder what it might be like if Regan did mean the words, if she really did love him. Just as quickly, he reminded himself that she was marrying him because she wanted Exclusives—not him.

At the nudge to his right shoulder, Cole yanked his gaze over to Jack, who gave him a puzzled look, then palmed him a ring. Cole stared down at the slim gold band in his hand. Something inside him twisted painfully at the sight of that ring. It was Regan's wedding ring. The same ring that he'd slid on her finger twelve years ago. The same ring he had sweated two extra weekend shifts to earn the money to buy. The same ring he clearly remembered tossing into the trash can when she had offered to return it to him after ending their marriage.

The minister cleared his throat. "The rings please."

Cole placed the ring on the Bible next to a larger wedding band to be blessed by the minister. "Please repeat after me. With this ring I thee wed…"

"With this ring, I thee wed," Cole said as he slipped the ring onto Regan's finger.

After Regan repeated the ritual and the minister pronounced them husband and wife, Cole's head was reeling with unanswered questions. Why had she retrieved the ring he'd thrown away? And why had she kept it all these years? Was it possible that she really had loved him? That she loved him still?

Just as quickly as the thoughts came, he dismissed them. If Regan had loved him, she would never have chosen her father over him.

"I now pronounce you man and wife. You may *kiss* the bride," the minister said, and given the flush staining Regan's cheeks Cole suspected he'd missed yet another cue. He lowered his head and brushed his mouth against Regan's. Her soft lips yielded beneath his and all the questions and reminders running through his head faded. She tasted warmer, sweeter, than he remembered. When she parted her lips, heat exploded inside Cole, and he closed his arms around her. Desire licked through his veins like lightning. No other woman but Regan had ever made him feel this alive, awakened this fierce need inside him, made him want to believe in love and dreams and foolish things he'd sworn off long ago.

The clamp of Jack's hand on his shoulder brought him back to earth. Cole lifted his head, heard the burst of organ music signaling it was time for them to exit. "Ready?"

Regan opened her mouth, closed it, then simply nodded. Smiling at the dazed look on her face, he hustled his bride out of the church and into the white limo waiting at the curb.

And, as the car sped down the street, Cole stared down at their joined hands. He wondered again why she had kept the ring. But any questions would have to wait, he realized, as they headed toward the St. Claire mansion for the reception he had agreed to allow Liz to host there. Now he truly regretted giving in to Liz's request. Because the party hadn't even begun yet, and already he couldn't wait for the reception to be over.

Regan pasted on a smile for yet another photo. After spending the past two hours posing for photographs and accepting congratulations, her jaws ached from smiling and the expensive new shoes Maggie had insisted she buy to wear with the wedding dress were killing her feet. She shifted from one foot to the other, wishing she could slip out of the darned heels and go upstairs for a nice long soak in the tub.

"Think it's okay for us to sneak out of here yet?" Cole whispered.

With the question still ringing in her ear, Regan's pulse scattered. For the first time since she'd decided to go through with the wedding, she realized she hadn't given a lick of thought to anything beyond the ceremony and reception. The truth was she'd still been reeling from that sizzling kiss he had planted on her in the church when she'd been whisked away to the reception. And since arriving all of her energy had been channeled into getting through this evening. Only now did the full ramifications of her decision hit her. This wasn't just another party she was hosting, where she could bid the guests goodbye at the end of the evening, climb the stairs and crawl into her bed to sleep. And this wasn't just any night either. This was her wedding night. And Cole was her husband.

"Princess?"

"Yes?" she managed to say.

"Are you ready to go?"

Her heartbeat went from steady to frantic. Cole had been

true to his word and hadn't bothered her during the past two weeks. Which meant that they hadn't discussed things like sleeping arrangements. She knew Cole wanted her physically. And to be honest, she wanted him, too. The sexual chemistry between them was even stronger now than it had been years ago. But she was in love with him, while he…he had married her out of a sense of duty. How could she make love with Cole, knowing that he didn't love her? Knowing that the vows they'd taken had been a sham? She couldn't. And while she knew he didn't believe she meant for their marriage to remain one in name only, she should have dealt with the issue of no sex between them long before now. She stared at the winding staircase, thought of her room upstairs and the nice cozy bed. And she imagined Cole in it—naked, aroused, tempting.

"Princess, you okay?"

She swallowed. "Um…yes. But I'm sorry. I just wouldn't feel comfortable disappearing upstairs now while so many people are still here. I mean I would know that they would all be thinking that we were…that you and I were…" She huffed out a breath. "I can't."

A grin tugged at the corners of Cole's mouth. "Actually, I didn't plan for us to spend the night here. I made reservations for us at a hotel."

"But why? We can stay here. This house is so big, we don't have to worry about getting in each other's way."

He brushed his thumb along her jaw, and his touch sent a streak of heat along her skin. "We're newlyweds, remember? Even though we've told people we're going to take a delayed honeymoon, I think it would seem strange if we didn't at least go away for tonight. Don't you?"

He was right, of course. But the thought of a night in a hotel room alone with Cole sent another rush of nerves swimming in her bloodstream. "I suppose so. I guess I haven't given our situation much thought past the ceremony."

"Then I guess it's a good thing I did," he murmured. "Let's go."

"Wait! I need to pack a bag for tonight."

"All taken care of. I had Maggie pack something for you."

Regan slanted a glance to her friend across the room doing her best ice princess routine on Jack. She owed her friend one for keeping this secret, Regan decided. Then suddenly her annoyance with Maggie gave way to worry about what her friend had packed. While Maggie wasn't keen on marriage or men because of her parents' machinations to see her married off properly, she certainly hadn't had any qualms about shoving Regan down the matrimonial path with Cole.

Gently taking her arm, Cole urged her forward. "Come on. Let's find your aunt and say goodbye. You look like you're about to drop any second, and I know you're dying to get out of those shoes."

"My feet are just fine," she told him, miffed that he could read her so easily when she couldn't read him at all. "Besides, these shoes cost me a fortune, and I intend to get my money's worth out of them."

"Trust me. They were worth every cent you paid for them. You look delicious—right down to those pretty toes of yours," he told her in a whiskey-rough voice that sent shivers along her skin.

"Um, there's Aunt Liz," she said, her voice breathless, her body aroused. "Maybe we'd better catch her before she disappears into the gardens with Mr. Peterson."

By the time they'd said their goodbyes and were driving away from her home, panic was swimming in Regan's blood. She figured she had ten, maybe fifteen minutes tops, before they reached the hotel. So she began formulating what she planned to tell Cole when they got there—namely that they were not going to share a bed. Not even to sleep. She would offer to take the couch.

"Relax, princess. I'm not going to bite you," he promised. "Unless, of course, you want me to."

His words sent that earlier kick of desire that she'd managed to repress licking through her again. So much for relaxing, she thought. She was beginning to think she might never know what it was to feel relaxed again. Glancing up, she noted they were on the interstate and heading in the opposite direction of the city. "Where are we going? I thought you said you booked us a hotel room?"

"I did. I just didn't say which hotel."

"But…Cole, I thought you understood that I can't take any time off now. I have a lot of work that needs to be completed—"

"I do understand. And we're not going far. I'll have you home by tomorrow night in plenty of time for you to go to work on Monday morning. Why don't you kick off your shoes, tilt the seat back and try to take a little nap. You really do look beat."

She was more than beat. She was flat-out exhausted, both physically as well as emotionally. Toeing off her shoes, Regan adjusted her seat and leaned her head back against the soft leather. "Well, maybe I will close my eyes," she murmured. "But just for a few minutes."

Regan could have sworn she had only closed her eyes for a few minutes when the sensation that she was floating came over her. She opened her eyes, but instead of the lights from the interstate, she saw an endless night sky filled with stars and moonlight. Instead of the hum of the car's engine, she heard the sound of the rushing surf, tasted the salt in the air, felt the breeze on her skin. And instead of the smell of the car's leather, she was surrounded by the scent of Cole. Her arms were looped around his neck, her head lay against his shoulder, and he was carrying her across a long stretch of sand. "Cole?"

"Hmm?"

"Where are we?" she asked, not even bothering to lift her head or protest being carried. She didn't feel nearly as tired as she had earlier, but she felt a lazy peace she was reluctant to relinquish just yet.

"On the Gulf Coast."

Tensing, Regan lifted her head and stared into his gray eyes. "Why?"

"Seemed like a good idea. The last few weeks have been pretty stressful. I thought maybe it would do us both good to get away, relax, get used to being with one another." He stopped in front of a little cottage. "Do me a favor. There's a key in the inside pocket of my coat. Get it for me?"

Quickly she retrieved the key from his pocket, but it was impossible not to notice the hard muscles beneath her palm, the warmth of his skin through his shirt, the scent of spice and male that was Cole's alone. "You can put me down," she told him, suddenly realizing that she had allowed him to carry her from wherever the car was parked to the cottage.

"Can't. If I do, you'll ruin your hose."

Regan looked down, realized she wore no shoes. More disturbing was the fact that the wind had whipped the skirt of her dress up to expose her thighs, and from the expression on his face, Cole was enjoying the view. She shoved the fabric down. "It's all right. I'm not worried about my hose. You can put me down."

"Afraid not. It's customary for the groom to carry the bride over the threshold. You want to unlock the door?"

Regan knew she should remind him that they weren't an ordinary bride and groom, that this was no ordinary wedding night. But when he smiled at her, the words seemed to get stuck in her throat. She yanked her gaze from his and managed to get the key in the lock. When the door opened, he carried her inside and kicked the door shut behind them. The room was dark, but the curtains had been drawn open and moonlight streamed in through the windows. The dim light cast his face in shadow, but there was no mistaking the hun-

gry gleam in his eyes. "You can put me down now," she
said, clinging to the last shreds of her sanity.

For a moment, she thought Cole was going to ignore her.
And heaven help her, for a moment, she wanted him to. But
slowly, he lowered her legs. When her bare feet touched the
cool tile floor and she started to step back, his fingers
splayed across her back, and he urged her closer. Her hands
lay trapped between them, pressed against his chest. She
could feel the rapid thump of his heart beneath her fingers,
knew it mirrored her own erratic heartbeat. The hand at her
waist slid lower, cupped her bottom and tugged her against
his arousal.

A feral light flashed in his eyes, turning them silver.
"Princess," he murmured and then he lowered his head,
slanted his mouth against hers. His mouth was as hard as
the rest of him, and hot, hungry, demanding. His hands fisted
in her hair, sent pins scattering to the floor. She circled her
arms around his neck and responded to his demands with
demands of her own. Regan could feel herself shattering
beneath the onslaught of his kiss. Desire for him burned like
flames through her body. She wanted him. Loved him.

When Cole lifted his head, her breath came in sharp rasps.
So did his. He slid his thumb along the curve of her chin.
"I want you, princess," he whispered. "And you want me.
This was the one thing between us that was always right.
Always." He explored the arc of her neck with his mouth
while he moved one hand up to palm her breast. Her nipple
beaded, pressed against his hand. "Come to bed with me,"
he whispered fiercely.

Heaven help her, she wanted to. She wanted him with a
fierceness that shamed her, frightened her. And if she were
to make love with him now, knowing it was her body he
wanted and not her, what hope did she have of surviving
once he ended their marriage? It was the thought of losing
him again that had her senses clearing. "I'm sorry, Cole.

This was a mistake. I shouldn't have let things go this far. I can't do this.''

His body tensed, and she felt the movement with every fiber of her being. ''You don't mean that, sweetheart.''

''Yes, I do. I'm not going to sleep with you, Cole.''

''Why don't we see if I can get you to change your mind,'' he said softly, seductively while his thumb caressed her bottom lip.

''Is that why you brought me to the beach? To try to seduce me?'' she asked, amazed that she could even string the words together when her body throbbed from his kiss, his touch.

''Do you want to be seduced, princess?''

With searing honesty, she acknowledged that a tiny part of her did want to be seduced by Cole, while the rest of her felt shamed by that need. ''No,'' she forced the word past her lips and prayed he didn't recognize the lie. ''And I won't let you seduce me.''

To her surprise, his mouth curved. ''Was that a challenge?''

''No. It was a statement of fact. You are not going to seduce me, Cole.'' She paused, scrambling for something, anything to keep him from knowing just how vulnerable to him she was. ''Or is it your intention to force me?''

The smile died on his lips and he released her so abruptly, Regan stumbled back, nearly fell. She knew she'd been playing with fire, knew she was being unfair. She didn't fear Cole, never had. At least not physically. A sneer curved his mouth. ''Don't worry, princess, you can go to bed now without any fear that I'll bother you again. You have my word, I won't lay a finger on you.'' Spinning away from her, he stormed toward the door.

''Cole, wait. I didn't m—''

The door slammed closed behind him. Regan fumbled with the lock, finally got the door open then rushed out after him to apologize for the uncalled-for remark. But he was already gone, a solitary figure in the night moving quickly down the lonely stretch of beach.

Cole walked down the empty beach, not caring that wet sand coated his expensive leather shoes or that the incoming tide splashed saltwater on the legs of his custom-made tuxedo trousers. He didn't notice when the rain began to fall, or when the slow drizzle turned into a steady stream of icy water that ran down his face and over his body. Not even when lightning streaked through the sky and the wind sent waves rushing up to the shore to slap at his ankles did he pay any heed. He simply kept moving, trying to escape the memory of Regan—the way her body curved against his so perfectly, the feel of her satin-soft skin beneath his hands, the scent of flowers that lingered whenever she came into a room, the taste of her that remained on his lips. He wanted to escape that jolt of fear he'd seen come into her eyes. But most of all he needed to escape the accusation she'd tossed at him—because it had been too close to the truth. He *had* wanted to seduce her. He hungered for her to the point of pain. He'd tried to tame this need for her, told himself he should stick to his original plan of marrying her, pretending to be husband and wife until the baby was born and then walk away.

But dammit, every time he caught a glimpse of her or even heard her voice, it grabbed at him, made him ache. She pulled at something inside him, made him want to feel, want to believe in something that he'd been so sure was dead. Despite all her denials, Regan wanted him every bit as much as he wanted her. And God help him, because tonight, for the space of a heartbeat, he had been tempted to use her desire against her, to ignore her protests and make love to her until they were both exhausted and sated.

Even now, he still wanted to go back to that beach cottage and give in to the chemistry that had been sizzling between them for weeks. And because his need for her was still so fierce, Cole continued to walk, welcoming the sting of rain on his face as he moved headfirst into the wind.

Time and distance blurred. Cole wasn't sure how long he'd been walking or how far he had traveled from the cottage. He simply kept going. Not until he reached an outpouring of rocks slick with rain and impossible to cross did he finally stop. Only now did he notice that the stars that had been in the sky when he had carried Regan from the car to the cottage had vanished, swallowed up by the darkness. Lightning forked through the sky and was followed by the bark of thunder. The heavens seemed to split open and rain came rushing out as if a dam had burst. Deciding to take refuge in an alcove formed by the rocks, Cole slumped to the ground and leaned back against the rock wall. He stared out at the water, noted the roaring three-foot waves that came crashing to the shore.

"Some wedding night," he muttered, shifting his shoulders away from a particularly sharp edge of rock in an attempt to get somewhat comfortable in his bed of wet sand. Thinking of the bed where he had planned to spend tonight brought back images of Regan. He didn't want to think about her. He didn't want to imagine her snuggled up in that bed in the cottage, didn't want to wonder what she was wearing, didn't want to remember the scent of honeysuckle on her soft skin. Disgusted, he stripped off his tux jacket and threw it to the side and settled against the rocks again. Too tired to be miserable or even to think, he closed his eyes. But even as exhaustion claimed him, it was Regan's face that filled his dreams, Regan's green eyes that stared back at him, the sound of Regan's voice he heard calling his name.

It was to the sound of Regan calling his name that Cole dragged himself back from sleep.

"Cole? Cole, are you all right?"

He eased open one eye, closed it quickly against the glare

of sunlight behind her. Squinting this time, he angled his head so that he saw only Regan leaning over him, an anxious expression on her face. Unbound, her blond hair reminded him of gold silk, he thought, noting the way it framed her face and fell in loose waves down her shoulders and past her breasts. Cole swallowed. The cropped yellow-and-blue floral shirt she wore had been tied beneath those breasts, revealing several inches of smooth bare skin between the shirt and a pair of lemon-yellow shorts.

"Are you all right?"

He jerked his gaze from Regan's thighs up to her face. Her dark gold brows were knitted into a frown and those liquid green eyes were filled with worry. "Yeah, I'm okay," he muttered from lips that felt desert-dry and a mouth that tasted like sandpaper. Shifting to sit up, he groaned as something sharp dug into his back.

"What is it? Are you hurt?"

"No," he shot back. "Just sore and a little stiff." He rolled his shoulders and neck, could have wept at the tightness in the muscles. He started to scrub a hand down his face, but at the sight of his sandy palms, he settled for wiping them on his sand-encrusted slacks.

"You sure you're okay?"

"Other than the fact that I'd kill for a shower, a change of clothes and something to eat, I'm fine," he assured her as he shoved to his feet. Or at least he was as well as could be expected for a man who'd spent his wedding night sleeping on a beach—alone. Regan, on the other hand, looked as fresh as a daisy in that little beach number and far too tempting for his peace of mind. "What are you doing here?" he asked, irritated that just seeing her had started that ache inside him all over again.

"Looking for you."

He scooped up his ruined tux jacket and stepped out of the alcove into the sunlight. Despite the slight breeze, he felt the full impact of the summer heat without the protection of the rocks. He was also aware of Regan standing behind him. Even with the beach and salt air surrounding him, there was no mistaking her floral scent. Deciding he needed some distance, he retrieved the shoes and socks he'd apparently tossed out on the beach during the night.

"I was worried when you didn't come back to the room last night—especially after that terrible storm came up. I called the sheriff's office—"

Cole spun around. "You did what?"

"I called the sheriff. I tried to get him to send a search party out to find you, but since you weren't out in a boat and the car was still at the cottage, he refused."

"It's a good thing he did. You didn't have to worry I was going to leave you there. I would have come back for you."

"I wasn't worried about me. I was worried about you. I've been looking for you since daybreak and only found you now because I saw your shoes. I was so afraid something terrible had happened to you."

She sounded so darn sincere, he almost believed her. Hell, he wanted to believe her. Just as he'd wanted to believe her keeping her wedding ring meant she still loved him. But he knew damn well she didn't. The admission only fed his anger. "Afraid, princess? Or maybe hoping?" At the stricken look on her face, he swore. "I'm sorry."

"It's all right. I guess I deserved that after my behavior last night."

"No, you didn't," he told her, furious with himself for hurting her. He started to touch her, but stopped himself. Aside from the fact that he was covered in sand, touching Regan would only set off that churning in his gut again. He rubbed at the back of his neck, managing to grind in more sand. "Just because I'm in a foul mood doesn't justify me taking it out on you. I was cruel, and you didn't deserve that. I'm sorry."

When he started to turn away, she touched his arm. "I'm sorry, too, Cole. For what I said last night. I never meant it.

I know you would never force me to do anything I didn't want to do.''

He stared at her fingers—so cool, so smooth and as pale as milk against the dark skin of his forearm where his shirt sleeves had been rolled back—and grimaced at her confession. ''Don't be so sure of that, princess. We've been striking sexual sparks off one another from the moment I walked into your shop. I wanted you pretty bad last night, and I knew that you wanted me. Enough that for a minute I considered giving us what we both wanted.''

''For a minute, I wanted you to,'' she admitted, withdrawing her hand. ''That's why I lashed out. Because I was afraid I would make love with you.''

''Would that have been so bad?''

''For me it would have. I'm not casual about sex, Cole.''

''Despite what you obviously think, I'm not either,'' he countered.

''I wasn't being judgmental. I'm just saying that for me sex has to be more than just the physical act. There has to be the emotional side, too. Otherwise, I could never look at myself in the mirror again.''

''So what are you saying? If I dress things up and tell you I love you, then it's okay for us to make love?'' He was being unfair, Cole admitted. But he resented the fact that he wanted to give her the words, and was afraid that he could come to mean them. ''Is that what you want? For me to say that I love you to justify the fact that we want each other?''

Her eyes frosted over, and that stubborn chin of hers jutted out. ''What I want is for us to get through the next six months without either one of us doing something that we'll regret.''

''Then I'm afraid you're out of luck, princess, because it's already too late for that. But the good news is, you'll be able to look at yourself in the mirror because I intend to keep the promise I made you last night. No matter how much I might want you, nothing's going to happen. So don't worry. You're safe with me.''

Eight

She didn't necessarily like feeling safe, Regan decided later that afternoon as Cole exited the interstate in New Orleans and drove the Mercedes down St. Charles Avenue. Unfortunately, he had been right about it being too late for regrets. It was. Yet, in the span of her day-old marriage she had already managed to log quite a number of regrets—starting with the way she had handled things last night and again this morning. She also regretted letting her insecurities and hurt feelings make her defensive with Cole. But most of all…most of all, she regretted not telling Cole the truth this morning. That she loved him. That she wanted to make their marriage a real one. That she didn't want to be his temporary wife, but his forever wife.

Only he'd misinterpreted her little speech on the beach, and when he'd indicated that he regretted marrying her, she'd been so hurt that she hadn't been able to bring herself to tell him any of the things that were in her heart. And since then the two of them had spent the entire day together and had discussed the dozens of things regarding the blending of their lives until the baby was born. They might as well have had the Gulf between them. Cole had remained true to his word. He hadn't touched her—not even in the most casual way—even when they'd laid out the plan for their living and sleeping arrangements. She couldn't fault a single thing he had done or said from the time they had headed back to the cottage for him to shower and change. In fact, the man had been kind, courteous and unfailingly attentive for the rest of the day. A perfect gentleman in every way.

And she had been absolutely miserable.

"You're sure you wouldn't rather see the place tomorrow? I mean, if you're tired, we can wait."

Cole's question pulled Regan from her unhappy thoughts, and she shifted her attention to the man seated beside her— her husband. She still couldn't quite believe they were married again. She also couldn't quite fathom Cole actually living in New Orleans. Knowing Cole had bought a home here made everything seem more real, more permanent somehow. "I'm not at all tired, and I'm really anxious to see the house."

He turned the car off the avenue and traveled down a side street filled with smaller homes than the ones that lined the city's premier street. "Just don't expect too much. It's not anything like your place. I mean, it's not a showplace. In fact, it's just the opposite. Kind of small and ordinary by comparison, I guess."

"But you like it?"

"Yes. I like it."

And she could see why he liked it, Regan acknowledged when he stopped in front of a charming raised Acadian painted a soft blue with white shutters. A wooden porch stretched across the length of the house, complete with rocking chairs and leafy green plants. Beds of pink and white impatiens banked both sides of the stairs leading up to the porch. A lush green lawn that looked as though it had been spread out as a welcome mat was dotted with several gardens bursting with colorful blooms. The white picket fence that surrounded the property only added to its charm. Cole had been right. The place wasn't grand in size or appearance as her own home was, but already she adored it. More importantly, she recognized the house. "You parked right across the street from this house the night you asked me to marry you." And he had promised her then that he would buy her a home just like this one someday where they would live with their children.

"Did I?"

Regan wasn't fooled by the nonchalant response. Cole remembered just as she did. This house was important to him, special for some reason. She hadn't realized that twelve years ago. But she did now. The fact that he'd bought this particular house and had asked her if she would consider living here made her heart swell with hope. "Trust me, Cole. When a man asks a woman to marry him, she isn't likely to forget where it happened. Is that why you bought this house…because you knew we were getting married again and wanted us to live here?"

"Actually I bought the place as an investment about a year ago when it came on the market. I just never got around to doing anything with it before now," he said. "You ready to see the inside?"

Regan placed her hand on his arm, felt him tense at her touch. "Before we do, will you tell me why you bought this particular house?"

He remained silent so long, Regan resigned herself to the fact that he wasn't going to share his reasons with her. Which was no surprise since Cole had always kept so many things to himself. With the exception of his passion, he had shared very little of what he was feeling with her. The realization saddened her, and she acknowledged how foolish she had been to think that Cole might begin sharing his feelings with her now simply because she was his temporary wife.

"My mother used to work here when I was a kid. It was one of the houses she cleaned every week. I must have been about four or five at the time, but I remember sitting on that porch and waiting for her in the evenings sometimes," he began. "I thought this was the most beautiful house in all the world, and I promised myself that one day when I grew up, I would own a place just like this. And that someday I would have a family just like the one that lived here."

Something in Cole's voice, a yearning, tugged at Regan's heart. He stared at the house, a faraway look in his eyes. "Tell me about the family, the one that lived here. What were they like?"

"Happy. They were always laughing and hugging one another, having fun together. Sort of like the families you read about in storybooks, I guess. I used to enjoy watching them."

And he had wanted to be a part of a family like the one that had lived here, Regan guessed, which made her heart ache a little more for him. "Tell me some of the things you remember about them."

"I remember waiting on the porch one afternoon for my mother. It was winter, about a week before Christmas, and I was really excited because she had promised to take me to see Santa Claus when she finished. Between the excitement and the cold, I couldn't sit still. So I cupped my hands and pressed my face to the window to look inside. There was a fire burning in the fireplace that day, and to keep warm I pretended I could feel the heat from the fire."

"Did it work?"

"I don't know. I forgot about the cold when I saw the Christmas tree they were decorating. It was the biggest and most beautiful tree I'd ever seen," Cole said.

"Describe it to me," Regan said softly, wanting him to

continue, wanting to understand more about this complex man that she loved.

"It was huge. A spruce, I think. Really tall, almost touched the ceiling. And very wide, with thick, green branches. It seemed as though there were a thousand lights strung on it, and more ornaments than I could count."

"Was there an angel on top?"

"No. A star," he said smiling. "A big shining silver star. The man who lived here had a little boy around my age. He lifted him up and let him put the star on top of the tree. I remember watching the two of them and wishing I was that boy."

Regan thought surely if a heart could break, hers broke in that moment as she listened to Cole. She ached for him—for the lonely little boy he had been, for the lonely man he was now. And she ached to tell him he was no longer alone, that she was here for him. But she didn't say a word. Aside from the fact that she doubted that Cole would want her love or her empathy, she was afraid if she tried to speak she would start crying and be unable to stop.

"Pretty sappy stuff, huh?" he joked, as though embarrassed by what he had revealed. "But at five, I guess I was impressed by this place and the whole Christmas scene. I even asked Santa to bring me a daddy and a house just like this one for Christmas that year." Cole laughed, but there was no joy in the sound, and Regan's already bruised heart broke a little more. "Of course when good old Santa didn't come through, I was one angry dude until my mother sat me down and explained how everything worked. That there really wasn't any such person as Santa Claus. That it was all just a myth."

Regan swallowed back a sob as tears slid down her cheeks. She could so easily imagine the boy Cole had been, lonely and yearning for a father, staring through the window at the family inside and wanting to be a part of it, wanting to belong. No wonder he had been so insistent about them marrying and the baby knowing he was its father. Until now, she had never realized that it wasn't the stigma of illegitimacy that haunted Cole, it was the loneliness and not belonging, always feeling like an outsider. Why hadn't she seen it before? It had always been there. Even at the reception yesterday, she had noted the way he seemed to stand back, to keep himself apart and view the goings-on as though he were merely an observer and not a participant in the celebration. And hadn't Aunt Liz told her that his mother and stepfather had called to say they couldn't come because of other commitments with their children? Once again, Cole had been the one left out. He had been the outsider—not one of them, not a part of their happy, new family.

And what about her? Regan demanded. All those years ago when she had ended their marriage and had lied to Cole, saying she didn't love him in order to protect him, she had only reinforced the message that he didn't belong. Guilt lashed at her and held the added punch of hindsight. The tears continued to roll down her face freely now. She couldn't go back and undo those mistakes, she told herself. But maybe it wasn't too late to make up for them. This marriage and the baby they were expecting could be a second chance…a chance to prove to him he wasn't alone. That she did love him…that she and their baby were his family now.

"Enough of the ancient history," Cole said, shaking his head as though he were wiping away the images. "If you're ready, we might as well go—" He stared at her, alarm flaring in his eyes. "Princess, what is it? What's wrong?"

"Nothing," she fibbed, ruining her breezy comeback with a sniffle. She swiped at the tears on her face.

"Then why are you crying?"

She took the handkerchief he offered and dabbed at her eyes. "It must be my hormones acting up again. I warned you, I cry over the silliest things these days."

He eyed her skeptically as though not sure if he should

believe her. "I'll take you home. We can look at the house tomorrow. I knew this was too much for you. You need to rest."

When he reached out to turn the ignition key of the car, Regan caught his wrist. "I'm not tired, Cole. I swear it. And look, the tears are already stopping. I told you, it's just my hormones. They're all out of whack. It's one of the hazards of being pregnant. Now come on, show me the house like you promised."

"Please," she whispered when he hesitated. "It looks so lovely from the outside, I really do want to see what it looks like on the inside."

"All right. I guess we can take a quick walk-through."

The walk-through *was* quick since the house wasn't huge, but quite large enough for a family. Although it was a two-story and sported four spacious bedrooms, a large country kitchen, dining area, family room, study, library and three baths, it had a cozy feel about it.

"So what do you think?" he asked when they were back on the main floor in the family room.

"I think it's lovely," Regan told him. And she did. With just a few personal touches, they could make this a warm and welcoming home. "It's a perfect house for a family, Cole. I can see why you bought it."

"I told you, I bought it as an investment."

"Uh-huh," Regan responded. But she knew better. Cole had bought this house because he wanted a home. That knowledge gave her the little kernel of hope she needed to make her believe they did have a chance, that they could make their marriage work, that she could earn Cole's trust, maybe even someday his love. "So when do we move in?"

"You're sure you won't mind living here? I mean, I know it would make a lot more sense for me to move in with you, but I'm just not comfortable with the idea of living in your house—even if it's only for six months."

A sick knot formed in Regan's stomach at the reminder

of how little time she had to make things right between them, to make their marriage work. "I told you. I understand, and it's not a problem for me to move in here."

He looked around the room again. "I know you did, and I appreciate it."

"But?"

"But I guess I feel guilty for asking you to. After all, it's not exactly the kind of place you're used to."

"What's that supposed to mean?"

"I mean this place isn't in the same league as that mansion you live in."

"Did it ever occur to you that I might like living in a normal house for a change?"

"Actually, it hadn't," Cole admitted.

"Then I guess you don't know me as well as you think you do."

"Maybe I don't," Cole said, a smile tugging at his lips. "And it's not like you'd be leaving your home permanently."

"Right," she agreed, but in her heart Regan hoped that she would. She wanted a new home, a new life with Cole and their baby.

"All right. But all you have to do is tell me if there's something you don't like, and I'll change it. It's important to me that you feel comfortable here. And the baby, too. I mean later. You know, whenever he or she comes here, I want the baby to feel at home."

"Don't worry, your baby and I will both do just fine here."

"How can you sound so sure?" he asked as though surprised by her reply. "I mean there's hardly any furniture in the place, and you haven't even been here twenty minutes?"

"I can sound sure because I am sure. It's not the house or the furniture that makes a place a home, Cole. It's the people living in it. Your baby will be happy and at home

here because it's where you are." And so will I, she added
silently.

"You make it sound so simple."

"That's because it is simple."

But there was nothing simple about the prospect of sharing a home with Regan, Cole decided three weeks later. If
anything, it seemed to be growing more complicated by the
minute. The nights he'd spent at her house had not been
easy, but he'd been determined that no one know their marriage wasn't a real one for their sakes as well as the baby's.
Even in the enormous house, he had been far too aware of
Regan sleeping under the same roof with him to be able to
rest. Now that the furniture they'd selected had been delivered and most of the unpacking done, he couldn't help but
speculate how much more difficult it would be living in
smaller quarters with her.

Even worse than the temptation of having her so close
was the realization that she was getting under his skin. Not
just in a sexual way, although all the woman had to do was
walk in a room and he'd be rock hard and aching for her
like a randy teenager. No, she made him feel things. She
made him want things—with her, for her, for them. She'd
tackled the furnishing of the house with such enthusiasm that
he'd almost believed they were a normal married couple
setting up their first home and beginning their lives together.

But only a fool would buy into that scene again, he
warned himself. Hoisting the box marked Canned Goods
onto his shoulders, he shoved open the doors to the
kitchen—then damn near had a stroke at the sight of Regan
standing on top of the counter of the island stove, trying to
hang a pot on the overhead rack. His box hit the floor with
a thud. "What in the hell do you think you're doing?"

Regan jerked around and started to wobble. Cole raced
over to catch her. "I've got you," he said, ice-cold fear
running down his spine as he wrapped his arms around her

legs and lowered her to the ground. One of them was shaking, and he thought it was *him*.

"Cole, I'm all right."

He heard her mumbled assurance against his chest, but dammit, he wasn't all right. He held on to her, waited for the blood to stop roaring in his ears, for his heart to stop bounding in his chest. Finally, he eased his hold a fraction so he could see her face. "I thought you were going to fall," he confessed.

"I'm sorry I scared you. But I was only hanging one of the copper pots over the stove. And I was being careful, honest. I swear I would never do anything to jeopardize the baby."

The baby? He hadn't even thought about the baby, Cole realized. It had been Regan he had been worried about, Regan he had been terrified would fall and break her neck.

She rested her palm against his cheek. "Thank you for rescuing me though."

Now that his heart rate had returned to somewhere near normal, he became aware of her fingers on his skin, the smell of honeysuckle in her hair, the feel of her body pressed against him. And his pulse began another heated race that had nothing to do with fear and everything to do with wanting Regan.

As though she'd sensed the change in him, her fingers went slack on his jaw. She lifted her gaze to his. Her eyes clouded, and she arched her neck so that her mouth hovered just below his. He wanted to kiss her, to taste her, savor her sweetness, lose himself in her fire. And it was because he wanted her so badly that he forced himself to let her go. Releasing her, he stepped back and drew a measured breath. "I think it would be a good idea if you didn't do any more climbing. If you have any more pots that need hanging, you let me know."

She nodded.

"I better go finish unloading the rest of the boxes. Then maybe we should clean up and go out for dinner."

"Couldn't we just eat here?" she asked.

The last thing he needed, Cole told himself, was to spend the rest of the evening alone with Regan. At least at a restaurant, there would be other people around to distract him. "Wouldn't you rather go out?"

"No. I'd rather just fix something here. If you're willing to risk my skill in the kitchen."

His reluctance had nothing to do with her culinary talents. "Tell you what, we'll eat in, but I'll put something together."

What he put together was a simple baked chicken with new potatoes and fresh spinach. For dessert he moved them into the den where he served bowls of chocolate ice cream—to which Regan added, much to his disgust, slices of dill pickles.

Amazing, Cole thought as he settled back against the couch and cast a glance around the room. Already the place had a warm feeling about it…a feeling of home. His eyes strayed to Regan, and he couldn't help but wonder how much this fuzzy feeling had to do with the furniture and how much it had to do with Regan being here with him. A hint of a smile played at the edges of her mouth, and her eyes were full of sass. She looked…contented, happy. And he could almost buy into the idea of them as a real couple.

"Ohh," Regan groaned. "I think that last pickle might have been too much."

"Princess, you polished off half that jar of pickles, along with an entire pint of ice cream. Not that I'm complaining, mind you, because you weigh next to nothing. But that was no lightweight dessert you put away."

"I'm eating for two," she reminded him primly, then ruined it with a giggle. "And I'll have you know I've gained seven pounds since I got pregnant."

"Where? You're four months along and not even showing yet."

"That's what you think. Look." She lifted the ends of her shirt and pointed to the slight bulge in her tummy.

But it wasn't her tummy Cole's gaze had locked onto, it was the strip of bare skin just above the waist of her unbuttoned slacks. It was as pale as cream and looked just as smooth, and set all those hormones he'd been working so hard to keep in check to racing at a full gallop.

"As you can see," she said, smoothing her shirt down again. "I can't even button my pants and skirts these days. Before long I'll look like a moose."

"But a beautiful moose," he murmured, more to himself than to her.

She smiled at him, and Cole's stomach tightened. "Thanks. I'll remember that when I start to waddle." She sighed. "And speaking of waddling, I'm so stuffed, you may have to carry me up to bed."

The words were no sooner out of her mouth than Cole felt his body respond to the suggestion. From the rush of pink to her cheeks, she realized it, too. The temptation to scoop her up and carry her upstairs to make love to her was so strong, Cole grabbed the ice cream bowls in order to stop himself from grabbing her. "Speaking of bed, I moved your things into the master bedroom," he told her.

"Oh," she said and pushed herself up. "And which…where will you be sleeping?"

"I took the room at the other end of the hall. I thought maybe the room that adjoins it would make a nursery."

"You're right. It would. I can help you fix it up if you'd like."

She reached for the napkins and jar of pickles. "Leave that. I'll take care of it," Cole told her. "Why don't you go on upstairs and get ready for bed?"

"But you cooked. I should at least help with the dishes."

"It'll only take me a few minutes. Besides, the dishwasher does most of the work. Go on. You need your rest."

"All right." She hesitated a moment, then came over and brushed her lips gently against his. "Thanks again for dinner. It was wonderful. Good night."

"Good night," he replied as he watched her head for the stairs. He drew his tongue across his lips, tasted chocolate and the tang of pickle and felt the throb in his lower body again. Sighing, he headed for the kitchen and resigned himself to the fact that it was going to be another long night.

It had been another long night, Regan conceded, as she secured her hair at her nape with a blue-and-white ribbon. After more than a month of spending her nights tossing and turning alone in the big bed while Cole lay in the room just down the hall, she was quickly nearing the end of her rope. The man had been a brick, steady and solid, even when she'd been at her worst. He had catered to her outlandish food cravings, comforted her during her crying jags, mopped her brow countless times after Slugger leveled her with another bout of morning sickness even when those bouts had hit long past midnight. He'd been tender, caring and thoughtful, insisting they turn one of the rooms in the house into a work studio for her to make things easier when the baby's due day drew closer. And he'd been sweet, impossibly so the evening he'd come home loaded with enough stuffed animals and baby toys to open a store. Just remembering that look of uncertainty on his face when he'd realized he'd gone overboard made Regan's throat grow tight all over again. If she hadn't already lost her heart to him, she would have fallen in love with him all over again in that moment.

The problem was that she already loved him while he.... She didn't have a clue how Cole felt about her. Oh, he cared about her and the baby. She knew that. His actions spoke volumes even if he didn't say the words. But caring didn't necessarily translate into love. And what chance did she have of him falling in love with her and making their marriage a permanent one if each time they moved a step closer, Cole took another step back from her? What she positively didn't understand was why he kept taking those steps back.

Cole wanted her, just as much as she wanted him. Even if he had cared to, he hadn't been able to hide the fact that he still desired her physically. She saw it in his eyes when she caught him watching her, felt it in his body's response when she insisted on giving him those good-morning and good-night kisses, felt it in the tightly leashed control she sensed in him whenever he held her close after a crying spell. Of course, he hadn't been the only one left breathing hard from their encounters. So had she. It was the reason she wasn't sleeping. Things had reached a point now where the slightest touch of fingers, an innocent brush of elbows, a quick glance across a room, was all it took to set off the sexual sparks.

Yet despite the fact that the heat they generated was bouncing like sound waves between them, Cole hadn't made one move toward doing anything about it. She'd tried giving him subtle signals that she wanted to make love with him—by stretching the ritual kisses from quick smacks to slow tastes, by reaching for his hand more often. Yet, each time she saw the blaze of hunger light his eyes, he withdrew, leaving her body and her heart aching. So what did she have to do, short of telling him straight out that she wanted him to make love to her?

If asked, both Maggie and Aunt Liz would say to tell him. But she couldn't. The world may have entered a new millennium, but she could barely think the words, let alone say them out loud to Cole. Which left only one choice—she had to seduce him. Regan glanced at herself in the mirror. The straight line of the white slacks she wore still revealed long, slim legs. The oversized powder-blue top with its boat neckline and three-quarter-length sleeves covered the pouch where Slugger seemed to be getting bigger by the day. Not exactly a femme fatale, she admitted. But with a little makeup, a slightly higher heeled shoe and with the help of dim lights, it might be enough.

It had to be enough, she told herself ten minutes later as she headed downstairs to join Cole for breakfast. "Morning," she said breezily, coming up behind his chair and looping her arms around his neck.

She felt him tense for a moment before he turned his head slightly and said, "Morning."

Deciding to take advantage of the situation and to practice her seduction skills, Regan kissed him full on the mouth. He hesitated a fraction, then his lips softened and he returned the pressure of her kiss for one long moment before drawing back. But in that quick smack, she had tasted not only the coffee that lingered on his lips, but something darker, hungrier that came from within the man. It was encouragement that she needed to go through with her plan. "So what kind of day do you have planned?" she asked, taking the seat beside him.

Putting the newspaper aside, he eyed her warily over his cup of coffee. "A pretty full one. I've got some contracts to go over and some financial statements to review on a hotel I'm thinking about making an offer on in Texas. I've also got a meeting with my broker and two bankers. Why? Is there something you needed me to do?"

"No, not really. But you said to let you know when I had my next doctor's appointment. It's today at four o'clock. I wasn't sure if you still wanted to go."

His face went solemn. "I'd like to go. I'll just need to rearrange a few appointments. Should I pick you up here or will you be at the shop?"

She really didn't need him to pick her up, since the dizzy spells had stopped right after her first trimester. But she wanted the chance to be with Cole. That's why she had purposely made the appointment late in the afternoon in the hope that he wouldn't go back to the office to work through the dinner hour and avoid her as he had been doing most of the past week. "Why don't you pick me up here? Then maybe we could get some Chinese take-out for dinner on our way home."

He groaned. "Please. Not fortune cookies and ketchup again."

She smiled. "Tell Slugger," she said, patting her belly. "He's the one behind the cravings."

"I'll try to remember that when I'm watching you eat and start turning green around the gills."

But Cole wasn't the one who turned green around the gills that night—she was. A fact which she hadn't counted on that morning when mapping out her plan to seduce her husband. She moaned and Cole wiped her brow again with a cool, damp cloth. "I've put the kettle on to make you some tea. You're sure you don't want me to call Dr. Lily or your Aunt Liz?"

"Positive. I knew I shouldn't have eaten that last fortune cookie."

"If you say so," he murmured, a grin playing at his lips. He caressed her cheek with his knuckles. The tenderness in his eyes, in his touch, as he sat on the couch next to her prone body, made Regan's heart swell. "Feeling better?"

"Yes," she whispered, loathe to have him stop touching her. "You sure you didn't mind us not finding out the sex of the baby today?"

"No," he replied, smoothing a strand of hair behind her ear. "Not at all."

"I'm glad. I sort of like the idea of not knowing until the time comes. Although, I've been calling this baby Slugger for so long I'm afraid if it's a girl she's doomed to be a tomboy."

"I can think of worse fates than having a beautiful tomboy for a daughter."

"And what makes you think your daughter is going to be beautiful? Most babies are pink and wrinkled and bald."

"Not this one. Not with you as her mother. She's going to be just as beautiful as her mother because it's in her genes."

A wave of tenderness washed through her at his words. "Thank you."

"No need to thank me. It's the truth. You are beautiful, princess, even more so now that you're pregnant."

Suddenly it was as though a strong wind had swept through the room. The light, teasing mood vanished and was replaced by a swirling heat that shimmered between them. Regan smoothed her palms up Cole's shoulders, felt the heat of his body beneath his shirt. He tensed but didn't say a word as his eyes locked with hers. Hungering for the feel of his mouth, the weight of his body against hers, Regan gave in to the aching desire and reached up, feathered her fingers through Cole's hair. She pulled him closer.

He resisted for the space of a heartbeat, and then making a sound part groan, part protest, he swooped down and captured her mouth with his. He took her with his mouth, his tongue, his teeth. There was nothing sweet or gentle or easy about this kiss. It was hot and hard and demanding—just like Cole himself.

Regan knew in her soul what she felt for this man went way beyond lust, way beyond the love of the girl she had been, way beyond what was safe or sane for a woman who was only a temporary wife. But she also knew it was too late for her to turn back. Even if she had wanted to, she didn't think she could. Cole owned her—heart, body and soul. And if she couldn't claim his heart, then at least for tonight she would settle for his passion. Her hands streaked over the hard planes of his shoulders, his back, his buttocks. She canted her hips, pressed against his erection.

He tore his mouth free. "Regan," he gasped.

When she reached for the buckle on his jeans, he snagged

her wrists, held them above her head with one hand and used his other hand to do some exploring of his own. And oh, how he explored.

When he slid his palm up her rib cage, Regan sucked in a breath that quickly turned into a moan as his hand journeyed higher and closed over her breast. He unhooked the clasp at the center of her bra with the speed of a man who knew his way around women's lingerie, Regan thought fleetingly. Then she couldn't think at all—only feel—as he shaped her, molded her, stroked her. When he captured one nipple between his teeth, heat arrowed straight to her womb. "Cole," she cried out his name and arched her back.

But already his oh-so-clever mouth had moved to her other breast and treated it to the same exquisite torture of alternately biting the sensitive tip, then laving it with his tongue. Just when Regan was sure she would die of pleasure, he slid his hand down her belly. He unfastened her slacks and cupped her. Regan lifted her hips, pressed herself against the heel of his hand and when he eased his fingers inside her, she felt herself come apart.

Nine

"Cole!"

"It's all right, sweetheart," Cole murmured as he stroked her, encouraged her, took her over one crest and then another. Her nails bit into his shoulders, and he had no doubt that she drew blood. Somehow the thought of Regan marking him with her passion fed into his own desire—a desire that had started smoldering the day he'd walked into her shop to demand that she marry him and had grown steadily ever since. Until now it raged like wildfire in his blood.

"Oh Cole, I...I..."

Something totally primal and inherently male took pleasure in hearing her sob his name as she shuddered and climaxed in his arms. He wanted to bring her up again first, watch her soar, see her shatter under his hand. Triumph shivered through him at the knowledge that it was his name she cried out, his hands and mouth that gave her this pleasure, his seed that grew inside her belly. Regan was *his*. She was *his* woman, *his* mate. She had been his since the first night she'd offered him her innocence and she was his again now. He wanted to claim her now just as he had claimed her that first time by sheathing himself within her sweet heat. But he held himself back, fearful of giving into that need, fearful of hurting her or the baby.

"Regan, no!"

Her fingers tore at his belt buckle, fought with the zipper of his pants. "Yes," she insisted as she freed him. She stroked his rigid length slowly until he thought he would go mad.

"This isn't a good idea."

"I don't care," she told him as her hand fisted around his swollen shaft. Cole groaned, and then suddenly he was the one trembling. He was the one ready to come apart at the seams. "Regan, wait," he rasped as she pushed him closer to flashpoint.

"I don't want to wait. I want you."

He grabbed her wrist, stilled her impatient fingers before she pushed him over that final ledge where he no longer had control over his mind or his body. Sweat rolled between his shoulder blades, down his chest. His body shook at the effort it took him to check his instincts to take her now as his body demanded. The air backed up in his lungs, and he struggled to breathe. "Princess," he pleaded when she tried to reach for him again. His breathing labored, he fought to hang onto that last thread of reason. "You've got to give me a minute. I want you too badly right now. I'll be too rough with you, take you too hard, too fast. I might hurt you…or the baby."

"You won't hurt me, Cole, and the baby will be fine." Then she gave him a smile that was pure female, the same smile he imagined Eve bestowed upon Adam before she offered him a bite of the apple. "Besides, maybe I want you rough," she told him, her voice a husky purr. Tugging her hand free, she ripped his shirt open, sent the buttons flying. With that siren smile still on her lips, she looked up at him with eyes that were pure sin and flattened her palms against his bare skin. "And maybe I want you hard and fast."

Something predatory in him leapt to life. Hooking a thumb in her slacks and panties, he stripped them away, exposing her completely to his gaze. Though he tried to control it, the animal in him took over. He took her mouth, savaged it, roared when she matched his hunger with a primitive demand of her own. The taste of his own blood sent heat firing through his veins. He tore his mouth free. Panting, he looked into eyes that mirrored the wild beat in his blood. He shoved his knee between her thighs, felt her slickness, felt her wet heat pulse against his leg. "I don't want to hurt you," he growled the warning.

"You won't. I want you, Cole. All of you. Fast and hard. Slow and sweet. Any way, every way I can have you."

Desire ripped through him with frightening speed at her words, and he grappled to rein in his fierce need. "I want to give you slow. I want to give you sweet. But I'm not sure I can, princess. I'm not even sure I know how."

"Then I'll help you," she promised and pressed soft kisses to his mouth, to his chin, to his chest. "I'll show you slow," she whispered as she eased her hand down his belly and closed her fingers around him. She opened herself to him, guided him into her wet heat. "And I'll show you sweet," she murmured as she lifted her hips to take him deeper.

Regan kept her promise. She showed him slow. She showed him sweet. Until each kiss, each flick of her tongue, each stroke of her fingers, drove him closer and closer to flashpoint. When he could wait no longer, he impaled himself in her fully and began to move inside her slow and sweet, then fast and hard, and faster and harder still. He grabbed her buttocks, held her tight against him and struggled for control. Then she wrapped her legs around his waist and arched her back.

He caught one nipple between his teeth. Her gasp of pleasure fed the fire inside him. She tangled her fingers in his hair and dragged his mouth to her other breast. And when he heard her cry out his name once more, felt her feminine muscles convulse around his manhood with the force of her release, Cole could wait no longer. He thrust into her one last time and followed her into the explosion.

It was the explosion of sound made by the screeching kettle that finally penetrated Cole's senses. With their bodies still locked together and the scent of spent passion swirling around him, he was reluctant to move. But at the persistent squeal coming from the kitchen, he eased his body from Regan's. She murmured a protest, and he captured her fingers, kissed them gently. "I'll be right back."

"Promise?" she asked sleepily.

"Promise." And because the sight of Regan lying there naked had him growing hard all over again, he covered her with the navy silk afghan that draped the back of the couch. After pressing a kiss against her head, Cole scooped up his pants and headed for the kitchen.

Moments later in the now-quiet kitchen, reaction to what had just happened between them and the consequences began to set in. As he poured hot water over the tea bag in the cup, his hand shook. Which about summed up how he felt. Shaken. More than shaken, he admitted. He was worried. Making love with Regan had just rocked the firm turf on which he'd always managed to keep his emotions under control. Somehow Regan had sneaked past all the locks he kept on his feelings and gone straight to his heart.

He had thought he could resist her, had thought he could pleasure her and not take for himself. But her passionate response had knocked him off his feet, cracked the very foundation of his control and opened all those doors that he'd kept shut for so many years. He scrubbed a hand down his face and raged at his own stupidity. He should have seen it coming, should have recognized his vulnerability where

Regan was concerned. How could he have been so blind? He had acknowledged months ago that he wanted her and had known that she had wanted him just as much. In his arrogance he had even concluded that in all likelihood they would end up making love and had set out to make sure they did.

Yet not even after that disastrous wedding night, when he'd realized that there was no way he could become physically involved with Regan without risking emotional involvement, had he recognized what a dangerous game he'd set in motion. He recognized it now. Despite his decision not to pursue a sexual relationship with her, it hadn't stopped him from wanting her. He'd accepted that fact, had told himself he could live with the desire that gnawed at him until the baby arrived and they divorced. But that was before tonight, before his plan fell apart. What a complete fool he'd been to ever think he could resist her.

Bracing his hands on the ceramic countertop, Cole stared at the darkening tea. Why hadn't he realized that he not only wanted Regan, but he needed her.

He didn't want to need her. He didn't want to crave her warmth, her gentleness, her passion. He didn't want to look forward to her unexpected kisses. To be tempted with her womanly smiles. To laugh with her over her silly food cravings. To have her feed the lonely ache in his soul that only she seemed able to fill. He didn't want to need Regan, but he did. And he didn't want to let her go.

But what choice did he have? She had never been his to keep.

It was ironic, Cole thought. He had gone through most of his life alone and managed just fine. Yet for the first time since he was a boy, he felt more than alone. He felt lonely. And it was a loneliness that went bone deep, one that he knew in his soul was going to be even worse when Regan was gone.

Because there wasn't a doubt in his mind that she would

leave. If life had taught him nothing else, it had taught him that Regan loving him was as much of a myth as Santa Claus. He'd stopped believing in Santa Claus that Christmas he'd awakened expecting to find a daddy and his dream house. Instead he learned that his father had never wanted him and that an unwanted bastard seldom lived in dream houses. He had about as much chance of Regan loving him as he had had of getting a dad and dream house for Christmas. Probably even less, he conceded.

And he had no one to blame but himself. Just as he had that night on the beach, he faced the truth—he had forced Regan into a marriage that she didn't want, a marriage that he had promised to release her from after their baby was born. Honor demanded that he keep that promise no matter how much he might not want to.

But sometimes honor sucked, Cole decided, as he returned to the den with Regan's tea. He placed the cup on the coffee table and moved beside the couch where she lay sleeping. She had fought her way from beneath the navy afghan so that it now draped over only a portion of her body, leaving her breasts, one hip and one long slim leg bare. With the moonlight spilling through the windows and the soft glow of the lamp shining on her, she reminded him of a pagan goddess lying there, her hair a swath of blond silk that tumbled down her shoulders and fanned over the couch. Her eyes were closed, and her lashes rested like dark shadows against her pale skin. That soft delicate skin bore the signs of his five-o'clock shadow, he noted with regret, and her mouth looked ripe and swollen. He lowered his gaze to her breasts. They were milk-pale, the skin so delicate he could see the faint blue veins that ran through them.

Cole sucked in a breath and swore viciously when he spied the marks on that perfect skin—marks he'd made with his beard and teeth. Guilt slicing through him like a surgeon's scalpel, he strode over to the window and stared out into the night. He should have taken more care, should have controlled his passion, he told himself.

Cole rubbed at his eyes, knowing he should regret making love with her but unable to do so. There was no question that it had been unwise on both their parts. Becoming lovers again only made things more complicated and would make their parting even more difficult when the time came. But the fact that they were lovers again couldn't be undone. They couldn't go back to the way things had been, and they couldn't go forward either because there was no future for them together. When the time came, he would have to let her go.

"Cole?"

He turned at the sound of her voice, and his body reacted at once to the sight of her holding the navy silk against her breasts, her cheeks flushed, her hair tousled. "I'm right here," he replied softly.

"I must have fallen asleep."

"Must have," he teased, drinking in the sight of her, wanting her all over again.

"I'm awake now. And I'm not feeling at all sleepy," she said in that low husky voice that had him growing hard again.

"I fixed you some tea," he said, determined not to succumb to his own selfish needs. He walked over to her. "If you're hungry, I can make you a snack."

She smiled that siren's smile at him. "Actually, I am hungry. But not for food."

So much for his good intentions, Cole thought, as his pulse kicked. "Is that a fact?"

"It's a fact."

"Then I guess I'll have to see what I can do to satisfy that hunger," he said as he lifted her into his arms and headed for the bedroom.

For now, it was enough that Cole wanted her, Regan reminded herself, repeating the litany she'd been saying for the past two months—since the night she and Cole had become lovers. She listened to the sound of the shower running in the bathroom, imagined Cole naked and wet. Recalling the night of passion they'd shared, she considered for a moment joining him, but her body felt too languid to move. Probably because she had gotten very little sleep, Regan admitted with a smile. After being out of town for nearly a week, Cole had been as hungry for her as she had for him. It seemed that absence really did make the heart grow fonder, she thought, then suddenly frowned because while Cole no doubt missed having her in his bed, he had said nothing about missing her.

Neither had she, she reminded herself. But then, last night she had had to bite back the words of love that filled her heart, just as she had done every night since they had married. And as each day went by, it was becoming harder and harder not to tell him that she loved him. Or to believe that Cole would soon realize that he loved her.

Sighing, Regan cut a glance toward the window. The first purple streaks of dawn chased through the darkness, bringing a new hope that this would be the day that Cole would finally unlock his heart and allow himself to love her again. But for now, she would cherish the present.

Because for now, Cole was still her husband—her attentive, considerate and passionate husband. Trying to count her blessings, Regan considered how much Cole had changed since that night he'd made love to her on the couch. He seldom worked late anymore and had often surprised her by showing up at her shop for an impromptu lunch or to kidnap her for a picnic in the middle of the workday or to take her on an excursion of some new baby boutique he'd heard about. Even in the routine things they did together—cooking, watching a movie or haggling over baby names—he seemed different. He made her feel special. And at night…at night he made love to her with a skill and generosity that staggered her. Quite simply Cole made her feel complete, happy.

And if asked, she would have sworn that she made him happy, too. He laughed more, seemed more relaxed, and he never left her with any doubt that he wanted her and found her attractive—despite the roundness of her body. Regan hugged the satin sheet around her. Sometimes at night when she lay in his arms, with her body sated from their love-making and the scent of him surrounding her, she could almost believe that they were a normal married couple in love with each other and anticipating the birth of their first child.

But other times, she thought as she heard the shower stop, other times she was forced to admit that they weren't like other couples. Slugger kicked, and she smoothed a hand over her belly. Other couples didn't have a clock ticking on their marriage that was scheduled to run out in three months.

The bathroom door opened, and her depressing thoughts vanished at the sight of Cole. He was naked, save for the towel draped low on his hips. A strip of light from the bathroom spilled into the semi-darkness of the room and lit him from behind, illuminating the long powerful lines of his body. Lord, but the man was beautiful, Regan thought as he moved with a lithe animal grace to the armoire. As though he sensed her watching him, he turned his head in her direction.

"I didn't mean to wake you," he said, his voice soft, gentle.

"You didn't," she assured him. "I was just enjoying the view."

His hand stilled on the door of the armoire. "Is that so?"

"Uh-huh."

"Then maybe you'd like a better view." He unhooked the towel at his hips, let it fall to the floor and started toward the bed.

Regan's mouth went dry as she watched him approach,

all rippling muscles and sinewy flesh. And very aroused male. Desire arrowed to her womb at the slow grin that spread across his mouth, at the hungry gleam that lit his gray eyes. "Very impressive," she said, determined not to back down from this sensual game they were playing.

"Glad you think so." He reached for the sheet she'd pulled around her body. Slowly, very slowly, as though he were unwrapping a gift, he peeled away the covering until she lay naked amidst the tangled sheets. His steel-colored eyes darkened, and excitement eddied along her flesh. As happy as she was to be pregnant, in that moment a streak of feminine vanity made her wish she could be beautiful and sleek and sexy for Cole. Aware of her protruding belly and the thickening of her waist, she used her hands to shield her swollen figure from his gaze.

"Don't," he said in a voice that had gone as smoky as his eyes. "I like looking at you."

"I look like a beached whale."

"You look beautiful…sexy…and very desirable. Please. Don't hide from me. Let me see you."

Regan hesitated a moment, then lowered her hands. Though the room was cool, suddenly she felt flushed, hot. Her skin tingled wherever his eyes touched her. Anticipation continued to build with each second that ticked by under his visual caress. When he lowered first one sun-darkened knee and then another on either side of her hips, desire careened in her veins.

With his sex, hard and hot, pressing against her belly, he fingered the tender skin around one nipple that bore the mark of his teeth from their lovemaking the previous night. Suddenly his mouth hardened. His eyes went bleak. "I didn't realize I'd hurt you."

"You didn't."

"I did," he corrected, his voice filled with self-reproach. "Just like I did that first time."

When he started to move away, Regan grabbed his wrist. "Don't. You didn't hurt me. I just have sensitive skin."

"I marked you," he shot back. "I lost control again."

"And I'm glad you did. I wanted you to. I wanted you to want me so much that you couldn't think, that you could barely breathe for the wanting. Because that's how you make me feel." Feeling brazen she ran her hands over the taut muscles of his shoulders, pressed her palm against the springy dark hair of his chest, and felt the rapid beat of his heart beneath her fingers. She lifted her eyes to his. "That's how much I want you now."

Desire flared in his silver eyes, sending shivers of heat through her body. Yet, despite the cording of muscles beneath her hands, his voice was tender as he said, "I promise I'll be gentle this time."

And he was gentle, impossibly gentle, as he kissed the corner of her mouth, her chin, her neck. He whispered kisses along her breasts, feather-light kisses that stirred the fire inside her. She could feel the tenderness with each brush of his lips against her skin. Curling her fingers in his hair, she pulled his head up and offered him her mouth. He slanted his head, fitted his mouth against hers. Regan tasted hunger in his kiss. She'd tasted that hunger before, reveled in the knowledge that his desire for her remained so strong. And she tasted remorse—which came as no surprise since he'd been furious with himself over a few marks on her skin from their lovemaking.

But what she hadn't expected to find in his kiss was the loneliness, the longing. Yet she did. It was the bone-deep loneliness, the yearning that clutched at her heart as nothing else could. When he lifted his head, for one brief moment Regan saw that same loneliness and yearning mirrored in his eyes. She wasn't sure how she knew, but in that one flash of insight Regan knew that this man that she loved with all her heart had no one else but her. Without her in his life, Cole would be completely alone. And while he might not love her, might never love her the way she loved him, she knew that Cole needed her in a way no one else ever had. Not her father. Not her aunt. Not her friends. Not even Exclusives. Cole needed her in a way no one else ever would. If there was never anything more, then this would be enough, she told herself. She would make it enough.

Love for him flowed through her. Fearing he wouldn't welcome the words, she tried to tell him with her mouth and her hands how she felt, that he would never be alone again because she was here for him, that she would always be here for him.

His sex pressed hot and hard against her belly, and she arched her back, wanting the feel of his mouth on her skin, the feel of flesh to flesh, wanting to touch him, to taste him, to show him how much she cared. But either Cole didn't read the urgency in her kiss or he ignored it, because he took his time and persisted in doing no more than kiss her. Soft, slow kisses that were driving her crazy. "Cole, I want…"

The words died on her lips as his mouth journeyed lower. Regan's stomach fluttered as his tongue swirled along her navel, then traced the roundness of her belly. Moving lower still, he made a place for himself between her thighs, then gently he opened her. The air stalled in Regan's lungs as he kissed the center of her womanhood. Holding her, when she would have pulled away from such intimacy, he stroked her with his tongue. She gasped at the incredible sensations hurtling through her, and, shamelessly, she lifted her hips for more.

Her body writhed, shuddered, beneath the onslaught of Cole's mouth. She could feel the pressure building inside her with each swipe of his tongue, with each gentle nip of his teeth against her sensitive flesh. "Cole, please. I—"

Spasm after spasm rocked through her. Yet he continued to drive her, to push her toward another release, and then another, each one more exquisite, more shattering than the one before. Another spasm slammed through her, and before she could catch her breath, he took her up again. This time toward some jewel-encrusted mountain peak that flashed in the sun like the rarest of diamonds, like the most precious of emeralds. And just when she thought she couldn't possibly bear the pleasure any longer, Cole thrust his tongue inside her again.

"I love you," she told him, just before the mountain exploded around her in a shower of brilliant diamonds.

Endless moments later the last of the shudders slowed. And the winking diamonds faded. Her vision and her mind began to clear from the powerful climax. Suddenly Regan's heart rate, which had almost returned to normal, sprinted.

Had she said the words aloud this time and not just in her mind?

A glance at Cole's face told her that she had. And that he didn't believe her. That he hadn't welcomed the words. It was there in the narrowing of his eyes, the taut line of his jaw, the utter stillness of his body. Since it was too late to take the words back, she told him, "It's true, Cole. I love you."

For one breathless moment, the words hovered between them like a shared heartbeat, and Regan prayed he would tell her that he loved her, too. A feral gleam came into his eyes, and he swept a hand along her hip, moved between her thighs. Brushing her hair away from her face, he said, "The truth is you want me, princess. And I want you."

Then his mouth was on hers, feeding hungrily, greedily, as though she were his last meal. His last hope. Regan gave herself to him, tried to feed the urgent need she felt in his touch, tasted in his kiss.

Pushing at his shoulders, she shoved Cole onto his back. Slowly, she eased herself over him. Glorying in the feel of him inside her, she began to move. Cole raised his legs to support her back while his hands palmed her breasts. Her breath came in pants now. So did his. She began to move faster, quickening the pace. She brought them closer, and closer still, almost to the brink of that jeweled mountain that Cole had taken her to earlier.

With a savage groan, Cole swept her beneath him and thrust into her. Anchoring her hips with his strong hands, he filled her and withdrew, again and again, each thrust sending them both closer and closer to that peak. She clung to him, roping her arms around his neck and pulled him into her body as she had already pulled him into her heart.

When the climax came, splintering the world around her, Cole crushed her to him and cried out her name. And for that one moment, with their bodies joined together and the world erupting into a million diamond lights around them, they were truly one—man and wife—as they were meant to be. Somehow, Regan promised herself, she would find her way back into Cole's heart before time ran out.

Ten

He'd made a lot of mistakes in his life, Cole admitted, as he sat in his office a few days later. And last night, lying in bed with Regan in his arms, with her head snuggled against his chest, he had come close to making another one. Just in time, he'd squashed the urge to tell her that he loved her.

Dammit, he didn't love her. He wouldn't allow himself to love her. He knew better than to let himself get suckered in that way again. If he did, then he would need her. And he didn't want to need her. Even though they'd been together for only a few months, already the thought of living without her made him feel dead inside. He didn't want to need her or anyone that way. And it would have been as much of a mistake for him to believe her when she'd said that she loved him.

But he wanted to believe her. So much so that he had ached with it when she had whispered that she loved him that first time. So much so that he still ached to hear her say it again. And he was scared spitless that when the time came and she had a choice, she would realize, as she had the last time, that she didn't love him after all.

His chest feeling hollow at the thought, Cole stared at the mountain of phone messages on his desk and the stacks of correspondence waiting to be answered. But even with the work piling up, he couldn't seem to think of anything or anyone but Regan. He squeezed his eyes shut a moment, and she was there again, looking up at him as she had the other night—with that dreamy look in her eyes, her mouth trembling as she said she loved him, her body so sweet and round with their child, her skin flushed as she welcomed him into her warmth. Opening his eyes, Cole gripped the arms of his chair as memories of their lovemaking came flooding back. Each time he buried himself deep inside her, he felt that he was home. That finally he had found the elusive place he'd longed for, searched for all of his life. The place where he belonged.

God, he was in deep, way too deep, Cole told himself, washing a hand down his face. Even the reminders to himself that he'd played out this scene with her before—the two of them married with a baby on the way and Regan swearing she loved him—only to have it blow up in his face, hadn't prevented him from hurtling heart-first into this maelstrom he had created. A maelstrom that had the potential to rip him to shreds.

And it would rip him to shreds. He had no doubts on that score. Because he had to let her go as he'd promised. He had to at least give her the option of being his wife because she wanted to be, without any threat or guilt hanging over her head. It was the right thing to do, Cole told himself, and he needed to do the right thing.

But doing the right thing didn't hold a heck of a lot of appeal. Not if doing the right thing meant he might lose Regan a second time.

The buzz of the intercom announcing Regan was there to see him jarred Cole from his brooding thoughts. He was out of his chair and yanking open the door to his office before she'd taken two steps. "Hi," he said, with a lightness he was far from feeling.

"Hi," she replied softly, almost tentatively. "I know you're busy, and I'm sorry to disturb you—"

"Don't worry about it." Brushing his lips against hers, he ushered her into the office and shut the door. One look at her face told him something was wrong and had fear knotting like a fist in his stomach. Bracing himself, he led her over to the burgundy-and-gray couch. "What's up?"

"I needed to talk to you. And I probably should have waited until tonight when you came home," she said, twisting and mangling the strap on her purse. "But I didn't want to wait that long to tell you."

"Tell me what?" Cole asked, his anxiety level kicking up another notch.

Tears filled her eyes, turning them a deep emerald green. "I…"

Cole eased down beside her, captured her nervous fingers in his. "Princess, whatever it is, you can tell me."

"I…you…we can't make love anymore," she blurted out, then burst into tears and flung herself into his arms.

He hadn't been quite sure what to expect, but Regan throwing herself into his arms and sobbing, deep, broken-hearted sobs wasn't it. Feeling helpless and hating to see her so upset, he patted her back, made soothing noises in an attempt to comfort her, not quite sure what to say or even what to do. Finally, when the worst of the crying was over and she lifted her head, he dabbed at her wet cheeks and eyes with his handkerchief. She sniffed, and he offered her the white linen to blow her nose. While Regan tried to repair the damage from the flood of tears, Cole made a dash to his desk to retrieve a box of tissues as backup. He set the box on the table, then eased her into his arms again. Stroking her back, he said, "Okay, now you want to tell me what's got you so upset?"

She pulled back a fraction and stared up at him. "Didn't you hear what I said?"

"Um. Yes. You said that we can't make love anymore."

She gave him an incredulous look. Instead of tears something akin to fury blazed in those green eyes. "And that doesn't upset you?"

Cole rubbed at his jaw, unsure how he should respond. "Well, I'm not sure that *upset* is the right word to describe how I feel."

"And just how *do* you feel?" she demanded.

"Disappointed," he replied honestly. Devastated, he added silently. "Princess, you're a beautiful, sexy and desirable woman and an incredible lover. All I have to do is look at you to want you. But sex wasn't part of our agreement, and I certainly don't expect you to sleep with me if it's not what you want, too."

Though she tried to hide it, Cole caught the tiny flinch, before she stood and walked across the room. She held her spine straight, but there was an air of defeat about her that made his chest go tight. "It isn't a question of me not wanting you. I think I've made the fact that I do pretty clear. But my doctor thinks that as long as I'm spotting we shouldn't—"

Cole's heart stopped. He felt the color drain from his face as fear jolted through him. In the blink of an eye he was reaching for Regan. "What spotting?" he demanded. "You never said anything to me about spotting."

A telltale flush of guilt stained her cheeks. "It started yesterday morning."

"Yesterday? And I'm just hearing about it now?" Not until she winced did Cole realize his fingers were digging into her shoulders. He loosened his grip, but didn't release her.

"I phoned Dr. Lily and went in to see her as soon as it started. She said occasional spotting wasn't uncommon during pregnancy and that I should just take it easy—which I did.''

Which explained her claim of being tired last night when he'd reached for her in bed. Fear riding him, his voice was harsh as Cole said, ''You should have told me. I'm your husband, and that's my child you're carrying. I had a right to know.''

''I know,'' she admitted, her voice little more than a whisper, her expression impossibly sad. ''But I didn't want to worry you unnecessarily…not after…not after what happened the last time.''

The last time being their first child that she'd miscarried. Suddenly all the anger drained out of him. He wrapped his arms around her, held her tightly. It was true, he had mourned the loss of their baby. And, God forbid, if Regan were to lose this child, he would surely mourn it, too. But it was the loss of Regan herself that terrified him most. And the realization that she mattered so much shook him. He didn't want to risk what caring that much could do to him. Unwilling to allow himself to think about his feelings for her, he pressed a kiss against her hair, inhaled the scent of honeysuckle, before easing her away so he could see her face. ''You're my wife, Regan. It's my job to worry about you. All right?''

She nodded.

''Does Dr. Lily want to put you in the hospital?''

''No. It's not that bad. She gave me something to stop the spotting. And the baby's not in any danger. I just have to take things easy for a while, and we have to refrain from sex,'' she explained, her eyes filling with tears once more.

''I knew you were working too hard at that jewelry store. I don't care what you say, I'm going to hire you some more help.''

''Cole, I don't need any more help,'' she insisted. ''Exclusives has been practically running itself ever since you convinced me to hire Sally to do PR and Jenny to help with the design work. Really. Not having to worry about running the store has been a relief. The truth is I already feel guilty because I'm spending my time doing what I love—the designs. And I have enough free time to spend with the baby when it comes.''

"So why are you so upset?"

She glared at him even as tears spilled down her cheeks. ''Because, you stupid man,'' she snapped. ''I've gotten used to being intimate with you. That's why. And now I have to get used to sleeping alone again.''

Cole narrowed his eyes. ''Let me see if I've got this straight. Because I can't have sex with you, you think I won't want to share your bed. Is that it?'' He didn't wait for her to answer as hurt and anger began to build inside him. ''Despite what you evidently think of me, I'm not an animal. And the only way I won't be sleeping in your bed is if you don't want me to.''

She broke into tears again, and Cole could have kicked himself for losing his temper. ''I'm sorry. I didn't mean to yell,'' he told her, gathering her into his arms.

She wrapped her arms around him as best she could with her bulging belly in the way. ''No. I'm the one who's sorry,'' she sobbed, her back heaving with the force of her tears. ''I thought you wouldn't want to be with me if you…if we couldn't…''

Cole eased Regan back a fraction, captured her tear-streaked face in his palms. ''I do want to make love with you. That isn't going to change. But if I can't make love with you, then the next best thing is holding you.''

''Really? You're not just saying that because I'm upset and—''

''Try to get it through that pretty head of yours, princess. I…'' Cole swallowed, realized how close he'd come to saying that he loved her. No, he wouldn't love her. He refused to let himself love her. He couldn't take that risk again.

''You what, Cole?''

''I…I care about you.''

* * *

I CARE ABOUT YOU.

Regan replayed Cole's words in her head again as she lay in bed beside him, his arm draped possessively around her middle, cradling her in his warmth. How many times had she replayed that scene in her head during the past month, she wondered. A dozen times? Fifty? A hundred? Too many times to count. And each time the word *care* struck her as wrong because Cole's every action, his every touch said that he loved her.

So why hadn't he given her the words? And why hadn't he told her that he wanted their marriage to be a permanent one? She'd given him several opportunities—complaining how huge her house would seem after living here, how lost she was going to feel in it—but he hadn't said a thing to her about staying with him. And with the clock on their marriage ticking down to less than four weeks, time was quickly running out. What was she going to do when the baby came if he still hadn't asked her to stay?

Just thinking of the alternative made her want to weep. Which was par for the course, Regan thought, shifting positions to ease the ache in her back that had plagued her all day. Listening to the steady rhythm of Cole's breathing, she closed her eyes and tried to sleep.

But ten minutes later, she gave up on sleeping. It simply wasn't going to happen. Easing Cole's arm from around her, she slipped out of bed, intent on going downstairs for a glass of warm milk with the hope it would help her sleep. She padded down the carpeted hallway and paused at the baby's room, unable to resist taking another peek. Smoothing a hand over her belly, she admired the results—the wallpaper of baby blocks in bright, primary colors, white bookshelves lined with storybooks with Mother Goose bookends, stuffed animals of every imaginable size and shape filling each corner, the bassinet and baby bed. She ran her fingers lovingly over the teddy-bear lamp that Cole had insisted they buy, and smiled at the sight of the baseball and tiny catcher's mitt he'd picked up on his way home from work one day. Cole was going to make a wonderful father, she thought as she turned away and headed down to the kitchen.

After she'd poured milk into a saucepan and turned on the burner, Regan pressed a hand to her lower back to ease the nagging ache that had started that morning and had grown progressively worse. The suspicion that she might be having more of the false labor pains that had sent them both into a tailspin last week flitted through her mind.

"Back still hurting?"

Regan glanced up and discovered Cole standing in the doorway. His hair was mussed, his chest and feet bare, his jeans unbuttoned and low on his hips. He looked rumpled and sexy and made every feminine cell in her body come alive. A stab of longing arrowed through her, reminding her it had been two months since they had last made love.

When the object of her lustful musing snatched the foaming milk from the burner, Regan flushed. She was insane, she decided with a smile. Here she was big as a house and less than a month away from delivering a baby, and she was lusting after her husband.

"Something funny?" Cole asked as he handed her the cup of warmed milk.

"I was just thinking that—" She gasped, her fingers tightening around the cup, as pain knifed through her.

"Regan, what's wrong?" Cole asked, his voice filled with alarm.

She sucked in a breath, and when the worst of the pain had passed, she said, "Slugger's practicing his karate kicks again. And that one was a doozy."

He frowned. "Are you okay?" he asked, leading her to a chair to sit down.

"Yes." But she worried her bottom lip with her teeth,

wondered if this was more of those false labor pains or the real thing.

"Why don't you finish your milk and then I'll give you another of my famous Thornton back rubs?"

"Sounds like a good idea," she said and started to get up when another sharp pain knifed through her.

"Of course it is, after all I... Damn. What's wrong?"

It took Regan a minute to get her breath back so that she could answer. "On second thought, maybe we'd better skip that back rub and get dressed. I think Slugger's decided to come a bit early."

Cole's face paled. His gray eyes grew frantic. "But he can't...you can't. It's too soon. You're not due for another three-and-a-half weeks," he screamed at her.

"Tell that to Slugger."

His eyes went from her face to her belly and back again. "Don't panic. Stay calm. You just stay right there, I'll take care of everything," he told her as he grabbed the phone and demanded an ambulance be sent—now. Leaving her standing in the kitchen, he tore out of the room and up the stairs. Moments later he was back wearing a shirt buttoned up wrong, pants and no shoes, and he was carrying the emergency bag they had packed for the hospital. "I've got everything under control. You don't need to worry."

"I'm not."

And she didn't worry—not when her water broke and she was sure Cole was going to faint. Not when she spent the next six hours in labor, with Cole holding her hand and telling her to breathe. Not when Cole cursed himself because he could do nothing to ease her pain. She didn't worry when Slugger finally made an entrance three weeks and three days early and turned out to be a healthy baby girl, weighing in at six pounds and four ounces. And worry was the farthest thing from her mind when Cole kissed her long and hard and thanked her for giving him the most beautiful daughter in the world. She certainly didn't worry when he flooded her hospital room with white roses and daisies and a big pink teddy bear. Nor did she worry when they decided to name the baby Elizabeth Mary after her Aunt Liz and Cole's mother.

Regan didn't worry at all until Dr. Lily told her that she and Elizabeth could go home. That's when she realized the terms of their marriage agreement were complete, and that Cole had never told her that he wanted her to stay. And that's when she was forced to admit to herself that maybe he didn't want her to stay.

"But there's no reason for you to go back to your place right away," Cole argued when Regan blind-sided him with the suggestion that afternoon after they had returned from the hospital and settled Elizabeth in the nursery.

"But we agreed after the baby was born, that I'd move back to my house and you'd start the divorce proceedings."

"I know what we agreed to," he snapped, feeling as though that magical carpet he'd been floating on since their daughter's birth had just been pulled out from under him. He knew damn well what he'd agreed to do, but that was before…? He refused to let himself finish the thought. He needed more time…time to prove that they were compatible, that they could make the marriage work. He shoved a hand through his hair and stared at the solemn face of the woman seated next to him on the couch. "The contract isn't carved in stone. There's no reason we can't be flexible. You're comfortable here, aren't you?"

"Very comfortable," she replied.

"And we get along pretty well together, don't you think?"

"Extremely well."

"So it would seem that the sensible thing is for you to stay here at least for a while. You just delivered a baby, and you need time to get your strength back, to let your body heal. And how will you do that if you go back to your house? The place is the size of a museum, and you don't have any family or staff there to help you. At least if you're here I can help. I could handle the night feedings so you could sleep—''

"I'm breast-feeding," she reminded him, a twinkle of amusement in her eyes.

Flustered, he said, "I can do other things...like bathing Elizabeth and changing her diapers."

She tipped her head to the side, a smile tugging at her lips. "Can I get that last one in writing?"

Cole scowled at her. "I'm being serious here, Regan. For you to go rushing back to your place so soon isn't a good idea."

"Then you want me to stay with you?"

He frowned. "Isn't that what I just said?"

"Not exactly. You said I needed to get my strength back."

"Well, you do. And with you living here, I can make sure that you do by seeing that you eat right, that you get enough sleep and don't overdo it. Your hands are going to be full with Elizabeth. You need someone to take care of you."

"And you're volunteering?"

"It's not a question of volunteering. You're my wife," he said, but he couldn't help wondering how much longer he could make that claim. It had been a long time since that night she'd told him that she loved him. And he couldn't help wondering if the reason she hadn't said the words again was because she'd realized, just as she had the last time, that she didn't love him after all. "You're my responsibility, Regan."

"Is that all I am to you, Cole? A responsibility?"

Something in her tone made him feel as though he were moving through a swamp filled with alligators, so he chose his words carefully. "What you are, princess, is a miracle.

My miracle,'' he amended, and because he needed to touch her, he cupped her cheek. ''You've given me the most precious gift a woman can give a man—a child. No matter what happens, you'll always own a piece of my heart for giving her to me.''

She closed her fingers over his hand, but she'd seemed to lose some of the sparkle that had been in her eyes. ''It works both ways, you know. I wouldn't have Elizabeth without you.''

''So are we agreed? For now, you and Elizabeth will stay?''

''For now, Elizabeth and I will stay.''

She and Elizabeth stayed, and by the time their daughter had been classified as perfect at her six-week checkup, Cole felt his life was perfect, too. Or almost perfect. While Regan had made no further mention of leaving, the possibility that she still might want to end their marriage hung over him like a dark cloud.

Careful to be quiet, in case Regan had already gone to bed, Cole eased open the front door then closed and locked it behind him. He listened for a moment to the silence before he headed upstairs in search of his two favorite females. He found them in the nursery. At the sight of Regan with the baby at her breast, Cole's heart stopped, then started again. He still couldn't believe this was his family, that he belonged to them, with them. How had he managed to live all these years without them?

As Regan cooed to Elizabeth, Cole's gaze shifted to her bare breast. Her breasts were fuller now, with a mother's milk, and the tips were rosy and damp from being suckled. Desire fisted in his gut. He wanted her with a desperation that bordered on pain, Cole admitted. He knew her body almost as intimately as he knew his own. And there hadn't been a night in the past three months that he hadn't lain in bed beside her, unable to sleep for wanting her. Oh, he understood the need for them to refrain from making love—first the spotting and then the healing from the baby's birth. But it didn't stop the want. It didn't stop the hunger that ripped through him each time he caught a glimpse of Regan.

As though sensing his presence, she glanced up, and their gazes locked. Heat bloomed in Regan's cheeks, and he lowered his eyes, watched her nipples harden. Desire clawed at him. He breathed deeply, willing his heart to slow, his pulse to even.

"Hi," she whispered as she placed the sleeping Elizabeth in her crib and re-fastened her top. "You and Jack finished your meeting early."

"He was in a hurry. Turns out he had a hot date with your friend Maggie."

Regan arched her brow. "That's a surprise. I know Jack claimed he was attracted to Maggie when he met her at our wedding, but I wouldn't have thought she was his type."

Cole chuckled as he walked with Regan to their bedroom. "Jack doesn't have a type. He likes women, period."

"Then I hope he knows what he's doing. Maggie isn't a woman who's easily taken in by a pretty face and charm. I'm surprised she agreed to go out with him."

After hanging up his jacket and tie, Cole said, "Jack and his family are loaded."

"So is Maggie. Her family's been tossing men in her path for years, and so far, she's managed to dodge them all."

"Then I say we let Jack and Maggie take care of their own love lives," Cole suggested as he watched Regan shed her robe. He nearly swallowed his tongue at the sheerness of her gown. In the dim light from the bedside lamp, he could see the shape of her body. Except for her breasts and a slight fullness at her hips, he would never have dreamed she'd only recently had a baby. The hunger that had choked him when he'd watch her nurse the baby gripped him again now. And it took everything in him to resist the urge to go to her, to cup her breasts in his hands and pull her against him. The need was so strong, he ached with it. Turning away, he dragged in a ragged breath. He'd promised himself he would wait, Cole reminded himself. As far as he knew, Regan hadn't gotten an okay from her doctor yet.

And even if she had, when he made love to her again it would be with no barriers between them. He was tired of wondering if she was with him because he'd black-mailed her into this marriage. He was tired of wondering if she really did love him. He was tired of worrying that she would walk out on him again.

Regan's arms stole around his waist. When she pressed a kiss to his back, the heat of her mouth burned right through his shirt to his skin. "Aren't you going to get undressed and come to bed?" she asked.

His body coiled tight with need, Cole forced air into his lungs. "In a minute. But first, I have something for you," he told her. Walking over to his jacket, he removed the canceled mortgage on Exclusives and turned to face her.

The look of anticipation on her face faded as he held out the envelope to her. "What is it?"

"It's the canceled mortgage on Exclusives. I should have given it to you weeks ago when Elizabeth was born as we agreed. I...I just never got around to it."

"I see," she whispered as she took the envelope from him. She opened the document, looked at it, then folded it back up and held it to her breast. "I guess this means I'm free to go now."

Cole felt as though she'd run him through with a knife. White-hot pain ripped through him. "I guess it does." And the thought of her leaving left him sick inside. He didn't want her to go, but he didn't know how to ask her to stay.

"I have some paperwork I need to finish for a meeting in the morning. You go on to bed. I'll be up later."

"Cole, I think we should talk—"

"It'll have to wait. I need to get to that paperwork." And if he didn't get out of there fast, Cole realized, he might very well drop to his knees and beg her not to leave him. The worst part of that scene, however, was that he was very much afraid she would leave him anyway.

Eleven

As Regan watched Cole race from the room, she slumped down onto the bed and hugged her arms about herself. She couldn't go on like this, she admitted. Maybe she had been kidding herself all these weeks—waiting, hoping Cole would tell her he didn't want to end their marriage, that he loved her the way she loved him.

Tonight when she'd looked up and spied him in the doorway watching her so intently, she had ached for him. Still ached for him. With her body. With her heart. And she had been so sure that he wanted her, too.

Obviously, she'd been wrong. Maybe Cole wanted to end the marriage after all. The idea cut through her like a knife, made her heart hurt so badly she pressed the heel of her hand against her chest to ease the pressure. The tears she'd been trying to keep at bay sneaked out and slid down her cheeks. She didn't want to let him go. She needed him. Their daughter needed him, and whether Cole knew it or not, he needed them, too.

Where's your backbone, St. Claire? Are you going to let him call the shots?

She could almost hear her friend Maggie's cynical taunt. Darn it, she wasn't going to let Cole go—at least not without a fight. She wanted him, and she wanted this marriage to work. Sniffling, she swiped the tears from her cheeks. A glance at the clock told her it was late to be calling Maggie, and she already knew her friend was out with Jack. But that was the beauty of answering machines and old friends, she decided and reached for the phone.

"Hi, Maggie. It's Regan," she said when the machine picked up. "I know you're out with Jack tonight, so you can call me back in the morning. But I need you to do me a big favor and keep Elizabeth for me tomorrow overnight. I'm planning to surprise Cole with a very special dinner."

And she intended to be on the menu, she added silently as she hung up the phone and began making plans to seduce her husband.

If she couldn't seduce her husband wearing this outfit, Regan decided as she viewed herself in the little black dress the following evening, then the title *woman* had been wasted on her. The simple black number had cost a fortune, but it made the most of her slightly fuller figure, softly cupping her breasts, waist and hips and stopping several inches above her knee. The matching black heels with tiny straps and silk stockings made her legs look a mile long. With her hair upswept and a few tendrils curling about her face and neck, she wore only her diamond studs and her rings. Her green eyes looked smoky, almost sultry, she mused as she checked her makeup one final time. Satisfied with her appearance, she checked the bedroom once more.

The room was a scene for seduction. The silver ice bucket sat in a stand near the foot of the big white iron bed, with a bottle of champagne chilling and two crystal flutes beside it. The soft green-and-ivory damask comforter had been

turned down invitingly and white rose petals lay scattered
over the sheets on the bed, their scent whispering through
the room beneath the gentle breeze of the ceiling fan. A
single white rose and daisy entwined with a slip of ribbon
rested beside each pillow. A glance at the clock told her
Cole would be home any second, so she quickly lit the candles that she had strewn throughout the room. Before heading downstairs to take the roast out of the oven and open
the wine, she swept her gaze across the room one final time.
Closing her eyes, she whispered a silent prayer that tonight
everything would go the way she had planned.

But two hours later when Regan finally heard Cole's key
in the lock, the roast was dried out, the potatoes were cold
lumps, and the wine more than likely was flat. The flicker
of alarm and irritation that flitted across Cole's face when
he saw her and the dining-room table set for two stung with
the force of a blow.

"I'm sorry I'm late. I got tied up."

"Too tied up to call or answer your cell phone? Too tied
up to try to come home when you promised me you
wouldn't be late?"

"I said I was sorry," he snapped, yanking at his tie. "You
should have eaten without me. There's a problem at my
office on the west coast and I have to handle the client personally. I'm booked on a flight that's leaving within the
hour. I just have enough time to pack and say goodbye to
Elizabeth."

"Elizabeth isn't here. She's spending the night at Maggie's," she told him, forcing herself to face the cold, hard
truth. It wasn't simply a matter of Cole not loving her. He
wasn't going to allow himself to love her. She sucked in a
breath at her own stupidity.

"Why?" he demanded, pausing midway up the stairs.

"Because I thought it was time you and I talked."

"I don't have time to talk now," he said, throwing her a

sharp look. "I told you I have a plane to catch. I'll leave a
number with my secretary where you can reach me if there's
an emergency. I'm not sure when I'll be back. Probably in
a couple of days."

Regan followed him into the bedroom he had slept in
during the early weeks of their marriage and watched him
drag clothes from the closet and cram them into a flight bag.
Suddenly the blinders she'd been wearing fell from her eyes,
allowing her to see the situation clearly for the first time.
Despite the fact that Cole had shared her bed for months,
he had never bothered to move his things into her room.
He'd claimed he didn't want to crowd her, to force her to
move any of her things to accommodate him. Only now did
she realize it had been just one more way for Cole to hold
a piece of himself back. She'd trusted him with her heart
and her body, but he hadn't trusted her at all. She couldn't
help feeling betrayed. And angry. "This can't wait a couple
of days, Cole. Book a later flight. We need to talk now."

He pulled open a drawer, grabbed a handful of handker-
chiefs and stuffed them in his bag. "What's so important
that it can't wait?"

"Our marriage. The contract on it expired six weeks ago.
I think it's long past time we decided what we're going to
do." She paused, took a steadying breath. "I want to know
if you intend to file for divorce?"

Cole suddenly went still. His expression bleak, his eyes
cool, his voice was filled with fury as he asked, "What's
going on, Regan? I thought you said you were happy living
here. Now you're telling me you want a divorce?"

"I love you, Cole."

"That's what you said the first time we were married.
And we both know how long that love lasted, don't we?
You'll have to forgive me if I don't put a whole lot of stock
in your claim this time."

His scathing reply clawed at her, but Regan held her

ground. "I do love you. I never stopped loving you. Why do you think I agreed to marry again?"

"You agreed to marry me because I backed you into a corner. First by threatening to fight you for custody of Elizabeth and then by buying up the mortgage on Exclusives. Love had nothing to do with it."

"That's where you're wrong. I married you for one reason and one reason only. I love you, Cole. But you won't allow yourself to believe that. Just as you won't allow yourself to love me."

"I stopped believing in love the first time you walked out on me, princess. I'm not fool enough to go that route again. It's bad enough that I still want you. That I care about you," he practically spit out the words.

"Wanting and caring aren't enough. I'm your wife and the mother of your child. I deserve more. I deserve your love and trust. And I'm not willing to settle for less."

He grabbed her by the arms, pulled her against him. She could feel the thundering of his heart beneath her palms, the thrust of his sex against her belly. "I want you." His mouth came down on hers in a bruising kiss. And when he lifted his head, his voice was as tight as his expression as he said, "I don't want you to go."

"Then give me a reason to stay." Holding her breath, she waited, prayed for him to say the words, prayed for him to give them a chance. Anger flashed in his silver eyes. And for the first time ever, Regan saw fear. Cole was afraid to love her. The burst of insight staggered her. He had always seemed so strong to her, so indestructible, and yet now she realized Cole was a vulnerable man because he needed and longed to be loved. And he was terrified of that need. Silence stretched between them and for a moment, Regan thought her prayers were going to be answered.

But Cole released her, took a step back. "I can't give you more than I have in me to give," he told her, his voice rough, empty. "I have to go. Will you be here when I get back?"

"Does it matter?"

His mouth hardened. After zipping up the flight bag, he slung it over his shoulder. "It matters where Elizabeth's concerned. She's my daughter, too. And this is her home. I want her to grow up here. With me. Whether you stay or not is up to you."

As he walked past her and out the room, his expression was as brutal and cold as his words had been…and sent pain slicing through Regan. And at the sound of the door closing behind him, the door of hope that she could break through the walls around Cole's heart closed, too.

Blinded by tears, she stumbled into her bedroom. The sight of champagne, the flickering candles and the rose petals scattered across the sheets brought a sob to her throat. Angry and hurting, she swiped the rose petals from the bed with the sweep of her arm, then sank to her knees on the floor and began to cry. Deep, soul-wrenching cries for herself. For Cole. For what might have been. But Regan never realized that in her burst of fury, she'd toppled one of the candles from the night table. Or that the flame was already inching its way toward the edge of the lacy curtain that fluttered at the window.

Cole stared at Regan's bedroom window as he sat in his car. Gripping the steering wheel, he laid his head against the hard surface and fought back the ache in his chest, the overwhelming sense of loss.

Give me a reason to stay.

Her words ripped at him. He lifted his head, and, for the space of a heartbeat, he considered going back. He wanted to go back, to promise her whatever she wanted so she would stay. And if he did so, she'd not only make a fool of him again, but he would break the promise he'd made to himself to do the honorable thing and let her go. Starting the car, he backed out of the driveway and headed for the airport.

I married you for one reason and one reason only. I love you. But you won't allow yourself to believe that. Just as you won't allow yourself to love me.

Her words haunted him as he sped down the interstate. Had Regan been right? Had she spoken the truth about loving him now, just as she had all those years ago when she'd come to him, swearing she had lied to protect him and begging him for another chance? And had his refusal to believe her been out of fear and foolish pride?

He'd never believed himself a coward, but Cole knew in that moment he was. And a stupid coward to boot. Because he did love Regan. God knows he'd tried not to love her, had tried to convince himself to let her go because it was the honorable thing to do. But honor had had little to do with it, he admitted. He was afraid. Afraid she'd toss his love back in his teeth as she had once before. Afraid of the blow her rejection would deliver to his heart and pride.

His head spinning with questions, he parked his car and headed for the ticket counter. Standing in line, he thought about all the days, months and years that stretched out before him. Time he would spend without Regan. What good was his pride and heart if he didn't have Regan beside him to laugh with him, to play with him, to love with him? And what good was his dream house without Regan to share it with him? Nothing mattered at all without her.

"Sir. I need your ticket."

Cole glanced up at the brown-eyed ticket clerk. "I beg your pardon?"

"Your ticket, sir. If you're booked on the flight to Los Angeles, I need your ticket. It's boarding now."

A smile broke out across Cole's face. "Thanks, but I just remembered I forgot to tell my wife that I adore her and I can't live without her."

"Then I suggest you hurry home and tell her," the woman said, a bemused smile on her face.

Flashing the clerk a wink, Cole said, "I think you're right."

And he intended to do just that, Cole decided as he raced through the airport concourse, reclaimed his car and sped toward home...toward Regan. His heart. His love. His life. He rehearsed his apology and his plan to confess what a stupid man he was as he zipped along the interstate. He'd get on his knees and beg her if he had to, Cole told himself. Pride, honor, nothing mattered. Only Regan.

His head and heart racing with all he wanted and needed to tell Regan, Cole didn't even register the fire trucks or the crowd gathered on the street until he was almost home and a policeman forced him to stop.

"I'm sorry, sir. You can't go through here," a uniformed officer told him.

"What's wrong?" Cole asked.

"House fire. A candle caught a curtain, and the place went up like a matchstick. A shame, too. It was one of those pretty Acadians. All wood and—"

Cole was out of the car and fighting his way through the crowd before the cop could stop him. His blood turned to ice at the sight of ugly orange flames licking through his house, the worst of it in Regan's bedroom. An anguished animal cry rent the air and he realized it came from him. As he fought his way toward the house, his every thought, his only thought was of Regan.

"Hey, buddy. You can't go in there."

Cole tore himself free of the firefighter's grip and started for the house. Two other men grabbed him. "Let me go. My wife's in there. I've got to get to my wife!" Breaking free, he started for the house again.

"Cole! Cole!"

He whipped around, searching for Regan. Then he saw her, and his heart stopped. He drank in the sight of her beside the open doors of the ambulance. She pushed away the oxygen mask the paramedic was trying to get her to wear. Her face and hair were covered with soot. Her nylons had huge rips in them. And he'd never seen anyone more beautiful in his life. He rushed over to her, pulled her into his arms and held her in a crushing grip until he could stop shaking.

"Cole," she said his name in a raspy voice. "Cole, darling, I can't breathe."

He loosened his hold, but didn't let her go, just held her close, his fist clutched in her hair. "Are you all right?" he asked, his voice breaking.

"Yes," she whispered.

"Thank God," he murmured and kissed her smoke-scented hair. "Thank God. I was so afraid I'd lost you."

She pushed at his shoulders, and when he eased back a fraction, tears streaked through the soot that covered her face. "I'm so sorry, Cole. I was upset after you left. I was crying and fell asleep, never realizing I must have knocked over a candle. And when I woke up the bedroom was in flames and the house was filled with smoke." She sobbed. "I'm sorry. I've ruined your beautiful house."

"Shh. It's all right. It doesn't matter." He kissed the tears running down her cheeks. He kissed her eyes. And then he kissed her mouth with all the desperation and fear that had clawed through him when he had thought she was inside the house.

When he lifted his head, her eyes were dazed. Her mouth trembled. "I know how much that house meant to you. I'm so sorry—"

He kissed her again, this time tenderly, with all the love in his heart. "I don't give a damn about the house. The house doesn't matter to me. You're what matters to me."

"But it's your dream home."

He shook his head. "It's only a house. A very wise and beautiful woman once told me that a house isn't what makes a place a home. It's the people you share it with. I can always buy another house, but I can't replace you. I love you, Regan. You and Elizabeth are my home. You're the only home I'll ever want or ever need.''

Epilogue

"**I** can't believe it," Regan said as she stood with Cole in front of the house several months later. "It doesn't look like there was ever a fire, does it? Wait until you see the inside."

"Wait just one minute, Mrs. Thornton," Cole told her as she started up the stairs on the porch. After making sure Elizabeth was secure in her stroller, he told his daughter, "Now you stay put for a minute, short stuff. There's something Daddy's got to do." Then he scooped up his wife and carried her over the threshold and kissed her until they were both breathless. "Welcome home, princess."

Elizabeth, evidently none too thrilled to be left out of the fun started to fuss. "Put me down and go get your daughter before the neighbors come running to see what the noise is about."

When he and Elizabeth joined her again, Regan took his hand and steered him toward the stairs. "Don't you want to look at the downstairs first?" he asked.

"In a minute. There's something I want to show you first."

"The bedroom?" he asked hopefully.

She gave him a quick smack on the lips. "Later. First, I have a surprise for you." She led him down the hall and stopped in front of the door to the guest bedroom. "Remember how you told me I could make any decorating changes I wanted?"

Cole nodded.

"Well, I hope you don't mind," she said as she opened the door.

Cole stared at the Mother Goose lamp, the white bassinet and baby bed, the moon-and-stars nursery-rhyme motif. "It looks wonderful. But what made you decide to move Elizabeth's room?"

"I didn't," she told him, a smile curving her mouth. "Elizabeth is going to have the same room she had before. This one's for her baby brother or sister."

Cole stood stock-still as he let her words sink in. His chest tight, he stared at his wife, his love, his life. "Are you telling me you're pregnant?"

"Yes," she whispered. "And this time, my darling, Aunt Liz didn't have a thing to do with it."

Cole let out a whoop that made Elizabeth giggle, then swooped Regan into his arms and kissed her long and hard. And as her lips molded to his, Cole thought of his Christmas wish all those years ago and realized he'd finally gotten what he'd wished for—to be part of a family. Thanks to Regan, he was.

*   *   *   *   *

Multi-*New York Times* bestselling author

NORA ROBERTS

knew from the first how to capture readers' hearts.
Celebrate the 20th Anniversary of Silhouette Books
with this special 2-in-1 edition containing her fabulous
first book and the sensational sequel.

Coming in June

IRISH HEARTS

Adelia Cunnane's fiery temper sets proud, powerful horse
breeder Travis Grant's heart aflame and he resolves to
make this wild ***Irish Thoroughbred*** his own.

Erin McKinnon accepts wealthy Burke Logan's loveless
proposal, but can this ravishing ***Irish Rose*** win her
hard-hearted husband's love?

Also available in June from
Silhouette Special Edition (SSE #1328)

IRISH REBEL

In this brand-new sequel to ***Irish Thoroughbred***, Travis and
Adelia's innocent but strong-willed daughter Keeley discovers
love in the arms of a charming Irish rogue with a talent for
horses...and romance.

Silhouette®

Where love comes alive™

Visit Silhouette at www.eHarlequin.com   PSNORA

SILHOUETTE'S 20TH ANNIVERSARY CONTEST
OFFICIAL RULES
NO PURCHASE NECESSARY TO ENTER

1. To enter, follow directions published in the offer to which you are responding. Contest begins 1/1/00 and ends on 8/24/00 (the "Promotion Period"). Method of entry may vary. Mailed entries must be postmarked by 8/24/00, and received by 8/31/00.

2. During the Promotion Period, the Contest may be presented via the Internet. Entry via the Internet may be restricted to residents of certain geographic areas that are disclosed on the Web site. To enter via the Internet, if you are a resident of a geographic area in which Internet entry is permissible, follow the directions displayed on-line, including typing your essay of 100 words or fewer telling us "Where In The World Your Love Will Come Alive." On-line entries must be received by 11:59 p.m. Eastern Standard time on 8/24/00. Limit one e-mail entry per person, household and e-mail address per day, per presentation. If you are a resident of a geographic area in which entry via the Internet is permissible, you may, in lieu of submitting an entry on-line, enter by mail, by hand-printing your name, address, telephone number and contest number/name on an 8"x 11" plain piece of paper and telling us in 100 words or fewer "Where In The World Your Love Will Come Alive," and mailing via first-class mail to: Silhouette 20th Anniversary Contest, (in the U.S.) P.O. Box 9069, Buffalo, NY 14269-9069; (In Canada) P.O. Box 637, Fort Erie, Ontario, Canada L2A 5X3. Limit one 8"x 11" mailed entry per person, household and e-mail address per day. On-line and/or 8"x 11" mailed entries received from persons residing in geographic areas in which Internet entry is not permissible will be disqualified. No liability is assumed for lost, late, incomplete, inaccurate, nondelivered or misdirected mail, or misdirected e-mail, for technical, hardware or software failures of any kind, lost or unavailable network connection, or failed, incomplete, garbled or delayed computer transmission or any human error which may occur in the receipt or processing of the entries in the contest.

3. Essays will be judged by a panel of members of the Silhouette editorial and marketing staff based on the following criteria:

   Sincerity (believability, credibility)—50%
   Originality (freshness, creativity)—30%
   Aptness (appropriateness to contest ideas)—20%

   Purchase or acceptance of a product offer does not improve your chances of winning. In the event of a tie, duplicate prizes will be awarded.

4. All entries become the property of Harlequin Enterprises Ltd., and will not be returned. Winner will be determined no later than 10/31/00 and will be notified by mail. Grand Prize winner will be required to sign and return Affidavit of Eligibility within 15 days of receipt of notification. Noncompliance within the time period may result in disqualification and an alternative winner may be selected. All municipal, provincial, federal, state and local laws and regulations apply. Contest open only to residents of the U.S. and Canada who are 18 years of age or older, and is void wherever prohibited by law. Internet entry is restricted solely to residents of those geographical areas in which Internet entry is permissible. Employees of Torstar Corp., their affiliates, agents and members of their immediate families are not eligible. Taxes on the prizes are the sole responsibility of winners. Entry and acceptance of any prize offered constitutes permission to use winner's name, photograph or other likeness for the purposes of advertising, trade and promotion on behalf of Torstar Corp. without further compensation to the winner, unless prohibited by law. Torstar Corp and D.L. Blair, Inc., their parents, affiliates and subsidiaries, are not responsible for errors in printing or electronic presentation of contest or entries. In the event of printing or other errors which may result in unintended prize values or duplication of prizes, all affected contest materials or entries shall be null and void. If for any reason the Internet portion of the contest is not capable of running as planned, including infection by computer virus, bugs, tampering, unauthorized intervention, fraud, technical failures, or any other causes beyond the control of Torstar Corp. which corrupt or affect the administration, secrecy, fairness, integrity or proper conduct of the contest, Torstar Corp. reserves the right, at its sole discretion, to disqualify any individual who tampers with the entry process and to cancel, terminate, modify or suspend the contest or the Internet portion thereof. In the event of a dispute regarding an on-line entry, the entry will be deemed submitted by the authorized holder of the e-mail account submitted at the time of entry. Authorized account holder is defined as the natural person who is assigned to an e-mail address by an Internet access provider, on-line service provider or other organization that is responsible for arranging e-mail address for the domain associated with the submitted e-mail address.

5. Prizes: Grand Prize—a $10,000 vacation to anywhere in the world. Travelers (at least one must be 18 years of age or older) or parent or guardian if one traveler is a minor, must sign and return a Release of Liability prior to departure. Travel must be completed by December 31, 2001, and is subject to space and accommodations availability. Two hundred (200) Second Prizes—a two-book limited edition autographed collector set from one of the Silhouette Anniversary authors: Nora Roberts, Diana Palmer, Linda Howard or Annette Broadrick (value $10.00 each set). All prizes are valued in U.S. dollars.

6. For a list of winners (available after 10/31/00), send a self-addressed, stamped envelope to: Harlequin Silhouette 20th Anniversary Winners, P.O. Box 4200, Blair, NE 68009-4200.

Contest sponsored by Torstar Corp., P.O. Box 9042, Buffalo, NY 14269-9042.

PS20RULES

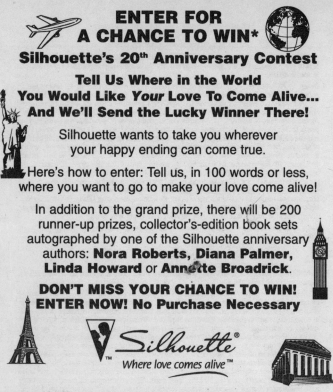

ENTER FOR
A CHANCE TO WIN*

Silhouette's 20ᵗʰ Anniversary Contest

Tell Us Where in the World
You Would Like *Your* Love To Come Alive...
And We'll Send the Lucky Winner There!

Silhouette wants to take you wherever
your happy ending can come true.

Here's how to enter: Tell us, in 100 words or less,
where you want to go to make your love come alive!

In addition to the grand prize, there will be 200
runner-up prizes, collector's-edition book sets
autographed by one of the Silhouette anniversary
authors: **Nora Roberts, Diana Palmer,
Linda Howard** or **Annette Broadrick**.

DON'T MISS YOUR CHANCE TO WIN!
ENTER NOW! No Purchase Necessary

Silhouette®
Where love comes alive™

Visit Silhouette at www.eHarlequin.com to enter, starting this summer.

Name: _____

Address: _____

City: _____ State/Province: _____

Zip/Postal Code: _____

Mail to Harlequin Books: **In the U.S.:** P.O. Box 9069, Buffalo, NY
14269-9069; **In Canada:** P.O. Box 637, Fort Erie, Ontario, L4A 5X3

*No purchase necessary—for contest details send a self-addressed stamped envelope to:
Silhouette's 20ᵗʰ Anniversary Contest, P.O. Box 9069, Buffalo, NY, 14269-9069 (include
contest name on self-addressed envelope). Residents of Washington and Vermont may
omit postage. Open to Cdn. (excluding Quebec) and U.S. residents who are 18 or over.
Void where prohibited. Contest ends August 31, 2000.   PS20CON_R2